OCEANOGRAPHY

OCEANOGRAPHY

STORIES BY JEREMY GRIFFIN

Ashtrah —
Thanks for reading!

ORISON BOOKS

Print ISBN: 978-1-949039-04-7
E-book ISBN: 978-1-949039-15-3

Orison Books
PO Box 8385
Asheville, NC 28814
www.orisonbooks.com

Distributed to the trade by Itasca Books
1-800-901-3480 / orders@itascabooks.com
www.itascabooks.com

Cover art: "Burn Season," copyright © 2003 by Shana and Robert
ParkeHarrison. Used by permission of the artists.
www.parkeharrison.com

Manufactured in the U.S.A.

ORISON
BOOKS

CONTENTS

For K and A

Birding for Beginners

1.

Two weeks after his wife's funeral, Sergio Paragioudakis, seventy-three, shambles into the back yard of his modest New Orleans row house and, using the leftover wood from the repairs made to the fence last month, builds a bird feeder. The design comes from a book given to him by Father Diamontapolous, *Birding for Beginners.* "This helped me when I lost my sister," the man said when he presented Sergio with the book; this was during *makaria,* the day after the interment. "Keeping the mind occupied, that is what is important. Idle hands, as St. Jerome tells us." Sergio accepted the book graciously, even though the idea struck him as a bit silly. A bird feeder. This was a child's project, not one for a grieving old man.

But now that his family has returned to their homes in other cities and the stream of mourners has diminished to the occasional casserole-bearing visitor, Sergio Paragioudakis finds himself alone for the first time in five decades and, as a consequence, his mind in desperate need of occupying.

It is late morning in June, and the humid air aggravates his arthritis, at first making the process painful and tedious. After a while, however, he finds himself enjoying a certain procedural rhythm—measure, cut, nail, measure, cut, nail. He has missed the satisfaction of working with his hands, manipulating parts into a whole. For forty years he was the owner and operator of Crescent City Vacuum Repair, on Canal Street, up until his second heart attack in 2009, at which point Luda demanded that he retire. "You have to take better care of yourself," she had pleaded. He wanted to argue that she was overreacting. After all, had he not already given up salt at her request? Did he not join her on a stroll around the block at least four nights a week? Even the doctor had commented on the surprising strength of his heart.

But when the woman you have spent three quarters of your life with is sitting next to your hospital bed dabbing at her mascara-streaked eyes with a Kleenex, gripping your wrist like a frightened child, you do not argue. All you can do is say *Yes, of course.*

Once the project is finished—a simple platform feeder with perching pegs and an A-frame roof—Sergio purchases a bag of seed from Home Depot and hangs the feeder from the lone dogwood in his back yard. Easing himself down into a plastic patio chair, he watches, waiting patiently for the birds to arrive.

Luda died on a Tuesday night, after a seven-year battle with ovarian cancer that included several extended periods of remission and enough maintenance chemotherapy to wither her down to a bony husk. The hospice nurse had estimated that she would not make it past Monday night. Once Father Diamontapolous was summoned to administer last rites, Sergio began mentally bracing himself for the moment that the last vestiges of life left his wife's frail body.

But then Luda did survive the night, much to the surprise of the brothers and sisters and nieces and nephews and cousins and friends who, for the past few days, had packed themselves into the small room of the hospice clinic. She was unresponsive to stimuli, practically vegetative—but still alive. "Sometimes they just hang on a little longer," the nurse said, trying to mask her irritation over having misestimated. "Guess she's a tough one." Among some of the elder family members, murmurs of miracles circulated, divine providence.

Sergio, however, much to his own disgust, could not bring himself to join in their delight. He had been in the room for nearly four days straight, listening to his wife's gravelly breathing and the tearful chatter of relatives he hardly knew, stepping out only for a few seconds at a time to speak to the nurses. And by Tuesday morning when Luda still had not passed, he found himself praying for her death. *Please just die*, he begged her inwardly. *This is enough. Just end it already, for all of us.* It made him feel vile and cold-blooded thinking such things, all the while knowing that it would surely cost him any heavenly mercy he might have hoped for in his own last hours of suffering, but still he prayed.

Around 10:30 that night, when Luda's stability was all but certain, he slipped out of the room to use the bathroom at the end of the hall. By the time he returned, she was dead. He had been gone no more than five minutes.

2.

A few days later, Sergio attempts another feeder, a hopper style this time with thin cylindrical walls to hold the seed and tiny slits at the bottom for access to the food. He purchases a pack of cheap model paints and stains the wooden base a sunny shade of yellow, Luda's favorite. Once the paint is dry, he hangs the feeder from one of the dogwood branches and again takes a seat in the patio chair like an eager moviegoer waiting for a show to begin.

Over the next few weeks, Sergio works his way through the book, attempting each feeder design—tube feeders, peanut feeders, suet feeders, nyjer feeders. As his stiff joints reacclimate to the work, his average construction time diminishes from an entire afternoon to a couple hours to only an hour. Each feeder he paints a different color so that they begin to look like a collection of oversized Christmas ornaments. Once he has exhausted all the designs, he begins developing his own, like a platform feeder with a thin wire mesh dome that, in addition to attracting scads of vibrantly-colored thistles, has the added benefit of keeping the squirrels away.

More birds congregate in the tree each day. Seated in the flimsy patio chair, sweating in the greasy Gulf heat, Sergio spends hours at a time with the book in his lap, trying studiously to identify each bird.

"That's a hell of a bird sanctuary you got there," his neighbor says one day over the fence, breaking his concentration. The fellow is stocky, thick in the face and shoulders, bald, with a silver stud in one ear. He only just moved in a few weeks ago with his son. The boy is hefty like his father, with dyed black hair that covers half his face and a perpetually churlish demeanor; Sergio guesses him to be about thirteen. This is the first time he has spoken with either of them.

"Yes," Sergio replies with a curt nod. "Many birds."

The fellow sweeps a chubby finger through the air. "You build all those?"

"I did."

"Damn. Those're nice. I'm kind of a handyman myself, actually." He gestures behind him to the motorcycle up on a hydraulic lift on his patio, a monstrous contraption with blue chrome fenders and tank. Many times Sergio has seen the man lying on the concrete beneath the vehicle, surrounded by an arsenal of toolboxes and cabinets, doing something to the engine with an acetylene torch. He rarely ever rides it, which is just fine with Sergio: motorcycles make him anxious, all that noise, always zipping about so recklessly in traffic (although admittedly these days it does not take much to frighten him behind the wheel; it has been over a year since he has travelled farther than the Megafoods a few blocks away).

"Built that thing piece by piece," the fellow boasts. "Took me about four months. Shoulda only taken two or so, but I do offloading at one of the Gentilly docks, and so I really only got weekends to work on it."

"Hm." Sergio nods.

"I'm Buzz Guidry," the man says.

Sergio sighs. "I am Sergio Paragioudakis."

The man—Buzz—clucks in the way that most people do when Sergio pronounces his last name. "Whoa, that's a mouthful. Say it again? Parajee, Para—"

"Just Sergio is fine."

"Alright then. Good to meet you, Sergio." They are too far away to shake hands, and Sergio does not want to leave his chair, so instead Buzz swipes his palm through the air in a *hello* motion.

"Yes, thank you," Sergio replies.

The man—Buzz—lingers at the fence as though waiting for Sergio to engage him in conversation. But Sergio is too absorbed in his bird watching to respond, and so finally Buzz taps the top of the fence, a gesture of finality, and says, "Well, I'll leave you to it, then."

"Okay, goodbye," Sergio says.

Buzz, he thinks derisively as the man lumbers inside his house. Such a name! Americans have no appreciation for the aesthetics of names. They scoff at Paragioudakis—derived from the surname given to an Anatolian priest who sheltered refugees during the Armenian Genocide—and yet they call themselves things like Buzz, the sound of insects. A person should not be named after the sound of insects.

Buzz and his son moved in shortly before Luda went into the hospice clinic, and so until now Sergio's interactions with the fellow have been limited to the occasional nod of greeting when they pass one another in their yards. At night sometimes Sergio can hear him and the boy arguing, their voices loud enough to elicit barks from the neighborhood dogs. The fights normally have to do with some misdeed on the child's part, though Sergio does his best to ignore them, more often than not turning the TV up to drown them out. Fortunately, they are usually short, often ending with the boy slamming the front door behind him and then pedaling off into the night on his rusted ten-speed.

3.

Early the following evening, just as Sergio is settling into his recliner to watch *Wheel of Fortune*, there is a knock at the door. He opens it to find Buzz standing there with his son. The man's face is screwed into an awkward smile, like a beggar preparing to ask for money. The boy gazes at the ground, his sleek black hair hanging dolefully around his eyes; Sergio sees that they are actually ringed with black eyeliner. God in Heaven, the boy is wearing *eyeliner*.

"Hey, man," Buzz says. "I hope you don't mind us dropping by like this. I just figured we should come by and introduce ourselves properly."

"Yes, okay, hello."

"This is my son Brian." He lays a meaty paw on the boy's shoulder. Brian sneers at the ground. Buzz clears his throat and licks his lips. "We've actually been meaning to come by for some time just to, you know, express our, uh, our condolences. For your recent loss."

"What's this? Express what?"

"Our *condolences*," he repeats, drawing the word out syllable-by-syllable. "We wanted to tell you that we are sorry. About your wife. Here, this is for you." He holds up an apple pie in a plastic container. *St. Anne Street Bakery* the label reads. "I'll be honest, I don't know shit about baking. But I swear to God, these guys make the best pies."

"Ah, well yes, thank you," Sergio says, taking the pie. "I enjoy pie."

On the day of the funeral, shortly after the reception, Sergio had been taking out a bag of trash when he spotted Buzz seated on a plastic milk crate next to his motorcycle, sipping a beer and tinkering idly with what appeared to be a carburetor. With the device resting on his large belly, he looked like a toddler fumbling with a toy. As Sergio was heading back inside, Buzz lifted his beer and offered him a slow, solemn nod, full of grim sympathy. Sergio had dipped his chin, an automatic response, and closed the door behind him.

Now Buzz bends down to whisper into Brian's ear. "You wanna say something, too, kiddo?" His voice is soft, though not so soft that Sergio can't hear.

Grimacing, the boy shrugs. "You just did."

"Yeah, but it'd be nice if you did, too."

"I don't know what to say."

"Just—come on, we talked about this. Don't be a prick. Just tell—"

"Sorry for your loss," Brian blurts with in the uninterested tone of a drive-through attendant. To his father, he says, "There, I said it. Can I go now?"

Sighing, Buzz offers Sergio an apologetic smile. He pinches the bridge of his nose. "Yeah, okay. Back by nine, though."

Without a word, the boy turns and slinks down the front steps and then slouches his way up the sidewalk, his hands crammed deep into the pockets of his baggy black pants.

"Sorry about that," Buzz says to Sergio.

"He is a nice boy," Sergio lies.

"Thanks. Honestly, he's a good kid, he's just been having a rough time lately." The man shuffles his feet and wipes the sweat off his forehead. To Sergio, he looks like a bashful adolescent working up the courage to chat up a girl. "Thing is, me and his mom split up a few months ago. Lorraine, that's her name. Long story, not pretty. I won't bore you with it. We're sharing custody right now, and Bri won't say it, but he's had kind of a shitty time with it." He winces self-consciously. "Sorry for all the language, by the way. Bad habit."

Sergio smiles and waves his hand: *It is okay.*

"Anyway," Buzz sighs, "I figured we'd come by, introduce ourselves, let you know we're here in case you need anything or whatever."

"Would you like to come inside?"

"Nah, thanks. I'm—"

"A drink? You would like a drink?"

"Really, I can't," he says, holding up his hands. "I'm doing a ten-to-six at work tonight. Couple of freighters coming in. They prefer us to be sober for that stuff, ya know?" He sniggers at this last part, and Sergio cannot help but grin. "But hey, maybe another time, yeah?"

"Yes yes, another time."

Later that night, during another unsuccessful attempt at sleep, Sergio thinks of his conversation with Buzz. The pie was just a pretense, he sees this now. It makes him feel bad for having been so abrupt the other day when the man introduced himself over the fence. It is just that he has never had the patience for idle chatter, not like Luda, who enjoyed striking up lengthy conversations with complete strangers in grocery stores and restaurants, much to Sergio's annoyance. "We do not know these people," he would hiss at her across the table, to which she would invariably reply, "That is the point."

If only she had been there today. She would have known what to do. She would want to bring them food, baklava and meatballs and beef stew with orzo. Grilled fish and homemade biscotti. Without a woman to look after them, Luda believed, men are as helpless as infants. Now, lying alone in bed, taunted by the ghostly silence of the house, Sergio begins to suspect that there is more truth to this notion than he thought.

After a while, he climbs out of bed and stumbles into the kitchen, where he pours himself a glass of water and, grabbing a used fork from the sink, sits down at the table with the pie.

4.

It is close to 3:00 on a Saturday when Sergio rings Buzz's doorbell. Brian answers the door, a can of Dr. Pepper in his hand. He is wearing the same black pants from before, the sides of which feature a network of seemingly pointless zippers, and a black tank top that offers minimal coverage of his burgeoning man-breasts.

"Hello," Sergio says too brightly. He has always been uneasy around children, but these inexplicably gloomy ones he sees more and more of these days confound him. "I am looking for your father. I am looking for Buzz."

"Ain't here."

"Ah, well." Sergio looks down at the bird feeder under his arm, a large tube feeder adorned with a sky blue conical lid made of hand-cut cedar tiles. "Do you know when he will return?"

The kid shrugs, takes a swig of his soda. "Don't know. He's at his Parents Without Partners meeting." He does not say the words so much as spit them out like something foul-tasting.

Sergio, beginning to feel foolish for having come by, frowns.

"You don't know what that is?"

"No."

"It's a bunch of sad old dudes sitting around feeling sorry for themselves and bitching about how they couldn't make their stupid marriages work." He lifts his chin toward the feeder. "That for him?"

"Yes, yes," Sergio says, perking back up. He hoists the bird feeder like a trophy. "A gift. For your family." He hands it over to the boy, puffing his chest out proudly, and then stands back and waits for Brian to thank him.

The boy turns the thing over in his hands, inspecting it as one might an appliance at a yard sale. He squints suspiciously at Sergio and takes another swig from the soda can. "Why do you always make these?"

Sergio cocks his head. Maybe he misunderstood him. Even now after so many years, he still struggles with English, all its pidgin dialects and nonsensical constructions.

"It is a gift," he repeats. "For you and your father."

"No, I get that, but why do you make these things all the time, is what I'm saying. I'm asking, like, why you do it." The boy belches into his fist.

Now Sergio is squinting back at him. He understands the question but not the context. *Why do you always make these?* As if he is being accused of something. So mistrustful, Americans, and for what? *The freest people in the world,* his father, a stone mason with seven children and a fifth-grade education, used to complain, *and still they look at each other like thieves.*

"I like to build things," Sergio finally answers. "I like the birds."

"But why?"

He knows the boy is taunting him, that he doesn't actually care about his interests. Belligerence is one of the less charming privileges of youth. Yet, as Sergio stares back at his black-ringed eyes, infused with a kind of challenging gleam, he finds himself unable to come up with a proper response. It is the simplicity of the question that throws him: *But why?*

Instead, Sergio clasps his hands in front of him and says once more, sternly this time, "It is a gift." Then, before the boy has a chance to ask any more questions, he plods back toward his own house. He hears the Guidrys' door close behind him, and he tries not to be bothered by the fact that the boy did not thank him.

5.

More feeders, more birds. Cardinals and mourning doves and bluebirds and wrens and jays. Sergio learns to distinguish their calls amidst the chorus of tweets in his back yard. The coarse squeak of the catbird, the thrush's watery trill. So many songs at once. Sometimes, if Buzz is working on his motorcycle, the two men will chat over the fence. That Buzz usually does most of the talking does not bother Sergio: he appreciates the company, the enthusiastic way the fellow talks about his motorcycle, like it is a sick animal he is nursing back to health. In fact, Sergio does not even mind whenever Buzz falls into wistful soliloquies about the dissolution of his marriage, a subject whose appropriateness he suspects he should question more than he actually does. (Apparently, his wife began seeing someone else while she and Buzz were still together; when confronted, she blamed it on Buzz's unreasonable work schedule, an accusation he does not necessarily deny.) How strange to think that for most of their twenty-year tenure in the house, Sergio and Luda had little use for the meager patch of yard, with its mangy grass and tufts of weeds and its dry gray soil. But now look at it, thriving with life and activity.

Yet, time and again he finds himself returning to Brian's question: *Why do you always make these?* What troubles him the most is not his inability to vocalize an answer for the boy but rather that the question needed asking in the first place. As if such a hobby requires justification.

Sergio had imagined that his wife's passing would send him into a debilitating state of grief, the same kind that had stricken Bette Carceros after her husband's stroke two years ago (the poor woman refused leave the house for three months—Sergio heard rumors of drug use and even late-night male callers but dismissed it all as the mindless gossip of housewives), and so he had prepared himself for the same thing. It was what had to be done. If age has taught him anything, it is that feelings are just *things*—manageable, guaranteed to change over time. After all, Bette did eventually emerge from her house, did she not? Indeed, she survived, and so would he. For, as it says in Matthew, "Blessed are those who mourn, for they will be comforted."

But Matthew said nothing about this—this nothingness that has plagued Sergio since that day in the hospital, when he returned from the bathroom to find his wife dead: a cold and hollow numbness that is somehow far worse than the crippling sadness he had anticipated, for it seems to belie the very notion of comfort. How does one manage an *absence* of feeling? The reassurances of friends and family, Father Diamontapolous' insipid jabbering about heaven and eternal peace and dwelling in the house of the Lord—what are these really but obligatory platitudes, well-intentioned but bereft of any real meaning? Comfort? Peace? Quaint fictions, nothing more.

But then there are the feeders.

Somehow they provide a sense of meaning and purpose. More than any sermon, more than the word of God Himself, they make Sergio feel productive, attuned to the world around him.

But of course, Brian Guidry cannot understand these things. How could he? He has never had to paw through his dead wife's clothes in search of a burial dress, has never had to sing the troparia, begging the same god that snatched her away—the one to whom she remained loyal and trusting her entire life—to at least offer her some form of rest in the afterlife, as if she did not already deserve this. No, Brian Guidry is just a boy, angry at the world in the way youth demands. Better to let him hold onto that anger for now. He will realize eventually the uselessness of such an attitude, that no matter how you feel about the world, it feels absolutely nothing in return.

Another late-night fight between Buzz and Brian. Sergio is half-awake in his recliner, the TV warbling mindlessly across the room, when he hears the telltale shouting. As usual, he can only make out words and phrases. He hears the boy say something about Jeff—Lorraine's boyfriend—and then his father respond with "Goddammit, I'm not Jeff!" A moment later the front door slams shut, and he knows it is Brian.

Wrangling out of the chair, Sergio moves to the window. He peeks through the curtains to see Brian walking past his house with his bicycle, his face half-hidden beneath the hood of his sweatshirt despite the heat. In front of Sergio's house, the boy pauses and kneels to examine the chain, which Sergio can see has come loose from the back gears. He fumbles with it for a minute or so until, in a sudden fit of frustration, he tosses the bike into the empty street, where it lands with an unceremonious clatter. Sinking down on the curb with his back to Sergio's window, he puts his elbows on his knees and lets his head hang despondently between his shoulders. From this angle, he seems at once childlike and impossibly old.

Briefly, Sergio considers going out to ask if he is alright—this is what Luda would want him to do. But if his previous dealings with Brian Guidry are any indication, it is unlikely that his concern would be well-received. And besides, he has always believed that it is rude at best and downright dangerous at worst to involve oneself in another family's squabbles.

Always these excuses, Luda might have argued, her voice dipping in pitch the way it did when she was angry. *He is just a boy, Sergio.*

But this, Sergio thinks, is precisely the point: what could a lonely old widower possibly offer the boy that he is not already poised to reject?

After a few moments, Brian heaves himself off the curb and retrieves the bicycle from the middle of the street. As he is turning around, he looks up to Sergio's window and catches him peeking through the slit in the curtain. It is only for the briefest of instants that they see each other, but it is enough time for Sergio to gauge the raging hopelessness in his tear-streaked face, and it calls to mind, oddly, the vagrants he used to see prowling the gutters and doorways near the vacuum shop, haggard old figures who carried their despair like nonfunctional appendages.

Quickly, Sergio shuts the curtains, feeling all at once dirty, as though he has witnessed something indecent.

6.

A few days later, Sergio walks into his back yard for his morning feeder-build, only to find the smashed feeders strewn about the yard. In a daze, he ambles about the yard, surveying the scene. It was the neighborhood children, he suspects, undisciplined delinquents that they are, the offspring of drug addicts and criminals. How many has he seen over the years carried away in police cruisers, young ones not even old enough to sprout facial hair? With this in mind, he cannot help but feel responsible, at least in part, for not having expected it.

In the tree, a handful of tiny birds no larger than golf balls hop from branch to branch, perplexed by the sudden disappearance of their village. Sergio feels a ridiculous urge to calm them. *I can build more,* he tells them in his mind. *Do not worry. I will make it right.*

He is several minutes into the task of gathering up the splintered pieces in the wheelbarrow when he comes across the sky blue lid from the feeder he gave to the Guidrys in a patch of grass near the fence.

7.

Buzz answers the front door. "Hey, Sergio," he says, "What's up?"

Sergio takes a breath. He has always lacked the heart for delivering bad news. "Your boy, he is here?"

"Left for his mother's this morning, actually. Her jagoff boyfriend picked him up. Why?"

"I believe he has broken my feeders."

Buzz tilts his head and scowls. "Bri did?"

"I believe so, yes."

"Well, um . . . " Buzz clears his throat. He crosses his arms over his big chest, making his muscles bulge. The posture of a man unafraid of settling disputes with his hands. "How do you know it was him?"

"I find this," Sergio says, holding up the blue pine-tiled lid. The feeder itself, or rather the pieces of it, are amongst the pile of remnants, but Sergio figured the lid would be sufficient to make his point. After all, he is not here to insult the man.

He guides Buzz outside and over to the fence. He points to the tree and then to the wheelbarrow nearby. Buzz turns the small wooden cone over in his thick fingers like Brian did when Sergio presented him with the feeder. He appears to be trying to make sense of the situation. After a few moments Sergio begins to wonder if perhaps he has explained himself improperly, another language barrier, until Buzz suddenly barks, "Goddammit!"

Flinching in shock, Sergio grips the top of the fence to steady himself.

"Sorry," Buzz says in a strained voice, rubbing his forehead, "I'm sorry, I'm just—oh man, I dunno what I'm gonna *do* with that fucking kid!"

Sergio breathes deeply, waiting for his heartbeat to slow down. He says, "It is okay. Children, they do these things." He holds his hands out in a *What can you do?* manner. "There is no harm."

"No, it's *not* okay, Sergio," Buzz replies through grit teeth. He is still staring at the blue feeder lid in his hand. "It's really goddamn far from okay. He knows better. This just isn't him. It's—it's like a different kid lately."

Leaning against the fence with his back to Sergio's yard, Buzz sinks down onto his haunches. Letting the lid fall from his fingers, he covers his face with his hands and sobs.

"I never thought it would be this hard, man," he says between phlegmy gasps. "I thought I could deal with it. But now I dunno know what I'm going to do. With Brian or with me or with anything. I'm just . . . I dunno."

Sergio looks around the yard as if a solution to the predicament might reveal itself. He is stunned into silence by the scene, this bear of a man bawling like a child, *because* of a child, no less. He wonders how Luda might respond, but for the first time in who knows how many years, he does not know.

"Come," he says to Buzz, patting his shoulder, "let us have a drink."

In the kitchen, Buzz takes a seat at the Formica table, which is covered with unopened bills and sympathy cards, while Sergio pours them each a glass of ouzo, two fingers apiece. They clink their tumblers and sip the cloudy white liquor, and when Buzz winces from the overwhelming sweetness of the drink, Sergio cannot help but smile. "Wow," Buzz says, licking his lips. "That's, uh, got a little sugar in it, huh?"

"You would like some water for it?"

"No, it's okay," the man replies with a wave of his hand. "Thanks, though. It's good, just sweeter than I'm used to."

Both men lean back in their chairs, taking small careful sips from their tumblers. The light from the window above the sink casts an uneven diamond on the wall above them. A few moments of quiet pass before Buzz says, unprompted, "He hates me." His voice is light and brittle in a way that tells Sergio he has been carrying this for some time, waiting for the right moment to unburden himself. "I mean, he seriously hates my guts. You know what he said the other day? He said he wishes I would just die so he never has to see me again. And it's like, what the fuck do you say to that? My wife left me, and now my son wishes I was dead and I can't do anything about it."

Sergio swallows, runs his fingers through his crown of thin white hair. He spent most of the cleanup in a furor, contriving an image of Brian creeping into his back yard at night, yanking the feeders down from their branches, and then stomping them to pieces, his chubby face screwed up into a devilish smirk.

However, now, watching Buzz Guidry stare down into his glass as though wishing he could crawl inside it, Sergio feels a stab of sympathy for the boy. He recalls the night he saw him in the street in front of his house, how he threw the bicycle onto the heat-moistened asphalt. That flash of helpless fury in his eyes. So much frustration and loneliness, and never anywhere to invest it. Our frantic attempts to reverse time, to salvage something worth understanding from the past—sometimes Sergio thinks this is all aging actually amounts to.

Outside, a car cruises past the front of the house blaring the kind of oonce-oonce rap music that always makes him think of the younger people at church, the second-generation folks whose refusal (or inability, perhaps) to feel obliged and burdened by tradition has always made him secretly envious. As the music fades to a distant thumping, Sergio says in a voice just above a whisper, "I was not in the room when my wife died."

It is the first time he has told the story aloud, and to hear himself do so feels dreamlike and surreal, not like speaking but rather like having the words pulled from him by some external force. Like praying, almost.

When he is finished, he tosses back the last sip of his drink and waits for Buzz to issue some hollow reassurance, perhaps something about the Lord working in mysterious ways—a phrase that Sergio has come to deplore for its hollowness, the way it exalts incomprehensibility as a virtue.

Thankfully, however, Buzz remains silent, looking pensively out the window toward his motorcycle.

Sergio stands and goes to the window. He has never really noticed how fierce the contraption looks, with its chrome mufflers and engine gleaming in the morning sun. Dangerous, but in a tantalizing way. "Tell me about this," he says to Buzz, motioning to the vehicle.

"What?"

"This, this motorcycle. Tell me about it."

Buzz stands and walks over beside Sergio. He leans on the edge of the sink. "What do you want to know?"

"What kind is this? Harley Davidson, yes?"

Buzz seems impressed that Sergio knows the name of the brand. "Yeah. An Iron 883. Blockhead engine with a Stage One kit."

"It is fast?"

Now Buzz is giving a Sergio a coy sideways look. "Yeah, she's fast. I mean, she's no speedster or anything, but for a cruiser, sure." He pauses, rocks back on his heels, the corner of his mouth bent into a curious grin. "Why you ask?"

Minutes later Sergio is sitting astride the back of the rumbling monster in Buzz's driveway, donning a German-style helmet. "I'll take her slow," Buzz tells him over his shoulder. "Just hold on." He revs the engine, and it is like holding tight to something on the verge of exploding, the heavy growl reverberating throughout Sergio's body, illicit and thrilling. As they exit the driveway into the street, Sergio cranes his neck to look again at the dogwood in his back yard, the scattering of birds lingering in the bare branches. The rest will return. He will build new feeders, yes, he will decorate the tree just as it was, but not yet. Right now he is taking his first ride on a motorcycle. He holds onto Buzz as they roar down the street, and he feels the heat of the bike beneath him and the sun and the wind on his face and it is like flying.

Robo Warrior

It is Sunday afternoon, and you have accompanied your mother to K-Mart to exchange the Robo Warrior* action figure that your aunt Leslie gave you several days ago for your eleventh birthday. The Warrior's name is Uppercut. His body is a kind of inverted pyramid with arms and legs that are almost gruesome in their musculature. He has a blonde flat-top and a blue skull tattoo on his right bicep, and his forearms appear to be sheathed in large silver gloves that reach up to his elbows. In theory, these are biomechanical replacement limbs composed of a titanium-platinum alloy. Their function is to maximize his efficacy in hand-to-hand combat. A small trigger on his back allows his hands to rotate a full three-hundred-sixty degrees at the wrist.

Biomechanical modifications such as these are hallmarks of the Robo Warriors*—a fact you well know, given that you are an avid fan of the cartoon series, now in its third season, and that you own roughly seventy percent of all available toy models (not including the four SuperMax Cyber Fortress* play sets, which, at almost sixty dollars apiece, just aren't worth the effort it would take to con your parents into buying them for you), including an Uppercut figure exactly like one that Leslie gave you. Out of politeness, you didn't point this out to her, though luckily she'd assured you that if you weren't happy with the toy, she wouldn't be offended if you exchanged it.

Your mother has agreed to bring you along on the condition that you not pester her about the exchange until she has completed her own shopping. Watching her wrestle a cart from the long train of them inside the doors, you can see just how exhausting the past couple days have been for her, all the giddy kid-birthday business. She looks like she's just woken up from a fitful sleep, her expression rigid and drowsy, her hair a riot of stringy wisps. In addition to the party at Splashtown! yesterday, where she sustained a mild sunburn on her cheeks and shoulders, there was also dinner at Camelot, the medieval-themed restaurant where the servers call you sire and serve you soda in enormous plastic tankards and stage jousting matches in the middle of the arena-like restaurant.

And so maybe it would be easier for you both if you just handled the exchange yourself. After all, you are eleven now. Practically a teenager. Surely that must confer upon you some new degree of responsibility. Only, she's got the receipt in her purse, and you'll need that when you go to the Customer Service counter, and you know there's no way she's going to let you do that by yourself, simply because that wasn't Part Of The Deal, and so instead, you ask if maybe you could at least go look at the toys while she does her shopping, *just look* you emphasize with the perfect degree of petulance, to which your mother, who you can tell is privately content to complete her shopping by herself, makes a show of sighing and rolling her eyes and then tells you okay, so long as you stay there and don't go wandering around the store.

According to the three-paragraph synopsis on the back of the package, the Robo Warriors' were created by the evil Dr. Z., a mysterious government scientist sent into exile after conducting a series of grisly biogenetic experiments on wounded American soldiers. The result of these experiments was an army of mindless cyborgs whom, through the neurocontrol chips in their brains, he was able to command from his secret laboratory in the South Pacific. Dr. Z. had come to believe that "modifications"—outfitting people with cybernetic components that would amplify their physical and mental aptitudes—was the next logical step in human evolution; he even went so far as to modify his own brain with self-replicating cyberneurons intended to boost his IQ.

Soon, however, a small number of Robo Warriors' discovered a way to disrupt the signals sent to the chips, thus freeing themselves from the doctor's hypnotic grasp, and the army splintered into two factions:

the Defenders and the Elite. The Defenders are the self-proclaimed protectors of all mankind against the Elite, who, under the control of the evil Dr. Z., strive for the assimilation of all human beings through cybernetic modifications.

Secretly, you've always been partial to the Elite, even though they are the bad guys. For one, their figures come with two weapons instead of one like the Defenders', and also their vehicles are flashier, more over-the-top, like the armored gyrocopter you got for Christmas last year, with its twin rotors and sleek chrome-like finish. But mostly it's because they don't spend every episode spouting clichéd good-guy phrases the way the Defenders do: "Mankind is already perfect, and you can't improve perfection"; "Friendship is the greatest weapon against evil." That you're-fine-just-the-way-you-are gospel is fitting in a typical cartoonish sort of way, but you've begun to realize that it doesn't hold up in real life. Because the truth is that mankind *isn't* perfect, and in fact most people spend their lives wishing they were anybody else at all, and so what rational person is going to pass up laser vision or indestructible synthetic skin or flame thrower hands?

This is what you're thinking about on your way to the toy section when your stomach begins to gurgle again from the King's Meal Cheese Fries you had last night—they haven't been sitting too well with you today. You make a detour to the restroom and duck into the first stall. Good places to think, public restrooms; you don't have to worry about making too much of a mess or using too much toilet paper or whether or not your dad is waiting outside in the hall with his copy of *The Wall Street Journal*. And lately you've had a lot to think about. Most of it has to do with your mother's reaction when you complained to her several weeks ago about how hard it's become to track down the Robo Warriors' you don't already have.

Maybe it's time to move on to something else, she said, pointedly unsympathetic.

Like what?

I don't know. I just think maybe you should try to broaden your perspectives a little. You're getting to that age.

You wanted to ask her what age she was referring to, but there was no mistaking the veiled warning in the statement, like age was something that required preparation, and you were afraid that pursuing the topic might steer the conversation in a much more serious direction than you were prepared for.

Now, sitting there in the smelly enclave of the stall, your thoughts drift back to your birthday party three days earlier: *Happy Eleventh Birthday* spelled out across the white cake in red icing thick as toothpaste. Double digits, you are double digits now. This, presumably, is a big deal. (The consensus among you and your friends is that ten, while technically a double-digit number, doesn't hold the same significance as all the numbers that follow it, largely because there's a zero in it—for all intents and purposes, ten is simply an extension of nine.)

For whatever reason, you had imagined that you would feel different by this point, more capable and sure of yourself. More like a grownup. But that hasn't been the case. If anything, you've begun to feel the exact opposite recently. Adrift, self-conscious, fearful in a dull, meandering sort of way. Your body has begun to feel like a garment you've outgrown, too tight in some places, uncomfortably loose in others.

As if to make things worse, your mother has begun leaving obscure little pamphlets from her church-sponsored Parents in Action meetings on the top of your dresser while you're out: *Your Body and You! Understanding Puberty!* Nearly all of the covers feature illustrations of teenage males with a baseball bat or a glove, their eyes fixed on the ground in attitudes of sober reflection. These illustrations are the reason you haven't given any of the pamphlets more than a single read-through, because whatever it is that is making those boys so depressed, you feel like you're better off not knowing.

Presently, your thoughts are interrupted by a sound in the stall next to yours, the rustle of clothing, the clink of a belt. You hadn't bothered checking the other stalls when you came in but had assumed all the same that you were alone, and the fact that you're not isn't really a big deal, except that after a few seconds you notice that the person hasn't flushed the toilet or even left the stall. There's just the sound of breathing coming from the other side of the partition, low raspy huffs. Heavy, but steady. Out of the corner of your eye you notice a shadow on the floor by your feet, and you look down to see that whoever is in there is kneeling on the grimy floor in order to angle his erect penis under the partition into your stall.

Actually, you don't immediately recognize the object as a penis, only because it doesn't make sense why someone would do such a thing. People don't just go around showing off their wieners to strangers. Or at least they're not supposed to, according to the police officer who came to your school last year to discuss the importance of not talking to strangers. Could the man have slipped and fallen while trying to buckle his pants? No, the contortion of his legs is entirely too complex, too calculated to be incidental, and plus, you would have heard it for sure. But then *why*?

Really, it should be funny. Penises are supposed to be funny. But in this case, it just feels like a cruel joke, the kind with a punch line that makes sense only to the person telling it. As a kind of test, you laugh, hoping that this might take some of the awkwardness out of the situation, but it's too nervous and uneven, which only reinforces the fact that you are more or less trapped there on the toilet with your pants around your feet.

The stranger begins stroking his penis. Slowly at first, almost experimentally, as though trying to familiarize himself with it, then faster and with more vigor. Snippets from the pamphlets your mother gave you are drifting up, unbidden, from your memory: *An erection occurs when a young man has sexual thoughts, which can cause the penis to become engorged with blood.*

As you sit there willing yourself to move, you instinctively recall the time that Todd Gilbride showed you his boner while you were swimming in his pool. His house is located in Hampton Courts, where each of the red brick estates has an enormous pool in the back yard, enclosed in a black iron fence and littered with colorful inflatable toys, like the neon green inner tubes that you and he took turns diving through. The trick was to get enough height off the diving board so that you had time to straighten out your body on the way down, allowing you to slip through the large ring with virtually no contact—a technique that Todd, a chubby boy with red hair and freckled cheeks that always make his face seem unwashed, could not seem to get the hang of. When he finally got fed up, he said *This is boring*, and paddled over to one of the water jets at the edge of the pool. With a toothy, malicious smile, he said *You wanna see something?* and then positioned his crotch directly in front of the jet. You knew what he was doing, you'd read about it in the pamphlets, *self-exploration* was how one of them put it, and you'd even tried it once or twice before, just a few harmless tugs on yourself to see how it felt, but you've always been too afraid to take it any further. Now, at Todd's, you tried to distract yourself by studying a ladybug floating legs-up in the water, but it was impossible to ignore his exaggerated moans, or his repeated cries of *Oh, baby!* just before he pushed himself away from the wall and leaned back so that his erect penis stuck up out of the water like someone's twisted notion of a buoy. He cackled, and so did you, even though you couldn't really see what was funny about it, and probably neither did Todd.

Sometimes erections can be embarrassing, but they are a perfectly natural part of growing up.

On the other side of the partition, the man shifts his legs and lets out another uncomfortable groan. Well, sure, it must be painful, kneeling backward on his knees like that. How long has he been down there, anyway? Hard to say, though the numbness in your feet and the cramping in your calves tell you that it's been at least a couple minutes. Another groan, this one strained in a way that makes you wonder if perhaps he has hurt himself, and then something lands on the floor next to your shoe, a small milky splat, and you're thinking about your Uppercut figure, those rotating fists, and how one day when you're older and have some money saved up you wouldn't mind getting a few modifications yourself, upgrading to more versatile components, replacing yourself piece by piece until the original you, the one to whom people seem to think it is okay to whip out their wieners, ceases to exist.

Then suddenly the stranger is on his feet and fumbling with his belt. He scrambles out of the stall, and you try to catch a glimpse of him through the crack in your stall door as he darts past, but it's just a flash of textures, hair and skin and a white t-shirt, nothing to distinguish him from anybody else.

After a few moments, when you find yourself able to move again, you pull your pants up and flush the toilet by kicking the handle, and you creep out of the stall into the dank bathroom. At the sink, your heart is wump-wump-wumping enough to make you lightheaded, and you have to steady yourself against the basin. You pump the soap dispenser for a dollop of pink goop, work up a thick lather under the scalding water. It's not that big a deal, really. So some guy showed you his wiener, so what? You know what wieners look like. And it's not like he touched you with it or anything. Get over it.

But still, why you?

Probably it was just a matter of chance. Your guess is that he'd been waiting in there for the next person to come along, and the fact that that person happened to be you was entirely coincidental. Even so, you can't shake the absurd suspicion that he sought you out specifically, that perhaps he recognized something in you that needed intruding upon, some piece of you that had gone unrecognized up until now, and so maybe this is why you refuse to look up at your reflection in the mirror as you frantically scrub your hands, because who knows what could be looking back?

Small islands of suds in the scummy basin. Ribbons of steam rising. *As long as it is done in private, "playing with yourself," otherwise called masturbation, is nothing to be ashamed of.*

Back out on the sales floor, the store seems somehow different, the overhead lights just a bit dimmer, the rows of vividly-colored merchandise dulled and diluted as though they have spent the past few weeks in sunlight. How long were you in the bathroom? Only a few minutes, but it's as if in your absence the place has aged drastically. Rounding the corner of the action figure aisle, you locate the Robo Warrior display: the stiff-lipped figures dangling from the metal hooks like prisoners in their transparent packages, waiting to be pitted against one another in an endless campaign of bedroom floor battles.

Except, no, something feels off. Where is the excitement, the capricious fervor that usually comes over you when you're in the toy section? In its place there's just a cold, sinking feeling, as though this is nothing more than a very convincing replica of the Robo Warrior display. For some reason, it makes you wonder about the Elite and their campaign to modify humanity. *Maximizing potential*, that's the phrase that Dr. Z is always tossing around on the cartoons, and the truth is that he may actually be onto something there, because it's not like anybody *wants* to be average, and it's not like any of the Robo Warriors' are worse off with their modifications. Of course, no one will ever acknowledge this, the same way they will never acknowledge the possibility that even good guys like the Defenders get it wrong sometimes, simply *because* they are the good guys, and therefore aren't afforded the luxury of change—not like actual people in the actual world, who are changing all the time whether they want to or not, getting taller and fatter and stronger and prettier and smarter and meaner, outgrowing themselves. Modifying.

And while you want to believe you're more than just your accumulated years, and that the things happening to you lately, to your body, serve some immediate function the way that mecha-fists or laser vision or arm-mounted RPG cannons do, something about the incident in the bathroom makes you wonder if you can even trust your body anymore. How is it even possible, knowing what people do with it? Just look at Todd Gilbride. Look at the stranger in the stall. Now look at you. Think about the kind of person you want to be, and consider how likely it is that you'll ever make it in one piece.

(You're getting to that age.)

Now here's your mother, rounding the corner with the cart. She smiles unenthusiastically, asks if you've made your selection, and it's all you can do just to meet her gaze.

I'll just keep it, you say.

But you said you wanted to exchange it.

It's okay. Can we just go? I don't feel good

What's the matter?

Can we please just go?

She's peering at you intently now, like she senses there is something you're not telling her, and you shift your gaze to the floor, the scuffed-up tile. Your poor mother. How is it even possible that she can be standing here with her arms resting on the cart handle, asking you about *toys*? She doesn't know that you're the kind of boy that strangers feel it's okay to show their wieners to in the restroom, and even though keeping it from her feels like a form of dishonesty, it's not like it's something you can explain, only because people don't talk to their mothers about wieners, everybody in the world knows that.

She steps around from behind the cart and crosses her arms and cocks a hip. What is it? she says.

You just shake your head, bite the inside of your cheek to fight back the tears.

Hey, look at me, she says.

But still you refuse to look at her. How can you? Instead, you hold the Uppercut action figure out to her like an offering—it doesn't belong to you anymore. She takes it, and then you close your eyes and give into the tears. You cry hard enough to make your body hitch and your chest feel as though someone is pumping the air out. Your mother stares at you, too confused to know whether or not you need consoling. She studies the action figure accusingly for a moment. What happened? she demands again, her voice now an even mixture of frustration and panic. Please tell me.

If only it were that simple, but no: you're in the toy section sobbing like a baby and all you want is for her to wrap you in her arms so that you can sink into her, be absorbed. You want to modify beyond the point of self-recognition. You want her to hold you tight enough to make you disappear.

Oceanography

1.

Brianna Copeland lies stomach-down on her beach towel, hoping she doesn't look as fat as she feels in her new swimsuit. When she came across the mint green two-piece on the Victoria's Secret website, she imagined herself as the model in the ad, all bronzed curves and windswept curls. Her fifteen-year-old figure, magically transformed. She didn't anticipate it making her look so hippy, the ruffled halter drawing attention to her stout frame rather than complimenting it as she'd hoped. Nor did she expect the color to clash so badly with her delicately freckled complexion. But by that point it was too late to send it back, and so now here she is on vacation in Myrtle Beach with the rest of the Copeland clan—mother Carol, stepdad Ray, brother Phillip—wishing she had never ordered the thing in the first place and counting down the seconds until she's back home in Raleigh. Back with Jump.

Up ahead at the shoreline her mother is trying to coax Phillip into the waves. "How about just one step?" she says, standing knee-deep in the surf. She clutches her monstrous sunhat to her head so that it doesn't go flying off in the breeze. "Can you do that for me, Bean? Just one step toward me?"

But Phillip isn't taking the bait. Instead, he crouches at the edge of the shoreline scouring the foamy sand for shells. "No, thank you," he replies mechanically, parroting the etiquette phrases they've gone over with the psychiatrist. His pasty back and shoulders are smeared with sunblock. At twelve years old, he's already cultivated an extensive roster of phobias, including water. Being near it is okay, but you try carrying him in, as Ray did a couple years ago at the rec center pool, and you're in for a shrieking, face-smacking meltdown. Sometimes it can take days to calm him down. Carol's *Managing Anxiety in Autistic Children* book insists that those fears can be overcome if Phillip can face them one step at a time, but Brianna wishes they would just let him hunt for shells in peace. It's his vacation too, isn't it? Let him do what he wants.

Besides, with the recent spate of shark attacks off the Carolina coasts, who can blame him for not wanting to go out in the water? Eight in the past two months, one almost every week, beginning with the kid in Wilmington whose arm got torn off from the elbow. Something to do with rising current temperatures, according to the bowtied expert on the local news. Brianna happened to catch the segment last week while flipping through channels. With the frail gentleness of an exasperated parent, he explained to the co-anchors that you still have a better chance of being struck by lightning than you do of getting attacked by a shark.

"You know, he might go in if you did," Ray offers, sprawled out beside Brianna in a plastic beach chair.

"I'm fine right here."

"It would be a nice gesture. To him and your mom."

"I don't see you going in, Ray."

He fishes around in the cooler for another Lima-a-Rita. Popping the tab with one hand, he takes a loud sip, a few droplets dribbling onto his furry chest. "I'm supervising this area right here." He flashes his *Ain't-I-so-funny?* smile. When he and Carol first started dating, he used to regale the kids with corny one-liners in an effort to earn their affections: "Didja hear about the fire at the circus? It was in tents!" Even at seven, Brianna couldn't help feeling that her mom should have been aiming higher.

Slipping in her earbuds and opening Pandora, she snaps a few more selfies to post on her wall, each one showing the faintest sliver of iris peeking friskily over her sunglasses while the wind tousles her hair. With any luck, they will be enough to grab Jump's attention. In the three days they've been here she has yet to hear from him, not a single returned call or text. Ordinarily she'd chalk this up to his distaste for cell phones ("Your fucking iPhone probably cost some poor Chinese kid his eyesight," he's fond of lecturing people), but after last week's confrontation all she needs is some reassurance that she hasn't ruined things for good.

After a few minutes, when the heat and the throngs of tourists have become overwhelming, Brianna announces to no one in particular that she's going back up to the room. She plods through the scorching sand toward the line of hotels running along the horizon. On the balconies, colorful towels and swimsuits flap like pennants in the salt-silky breeze. As she strolls into the Island Palms Resort, the blast of the AC, as well as a few involuntary glimpses from dads checking their families in, remind her how exposed she is, and she wraps the towel around herself. Part of her doesn't mind the appraising way that guys have started to look at her over the past couple years. And not just boys at school—cashiers and waiters and even some teachers, too, their lingering glances flitting over her body before redirecting themselves, embarrassed. But then there's another part of her that recoils at those glances, how they seem to discern things about her that she hasn't yet discovered for herself.

The only person who has ever made her feel genuinely pretty is Jump. At nineteen, he's a second-year senior at Brianna's school—though in his defense it's impossible for him to get a fair shake from any of the teachers considering they all know he runs with a gang of graffiti taggers. To them he's just a lowlife, a criminal in the making. They don't see him for what he is: an artist trying to pry people's eyes open to the "hypocrisy of consumerist culture," a phrase he wields as valiantly as a longsword. If they could get a look at his work, the sharp multicolored murals in alleyways and underpasses around town, they might finally understand him. Like she does.

After a quick shower, she hangs her damp suit over one of the slatted rubber chairs on the balcony and, resting her arms on the railing, peers down at the beach. Amidst the countless clusters of vacationers, she spots her family by the 71st Avenue lifeguard stand. Her mom has given up trying to lure Phillip into the water and is now reading a book in her beach chair while Ray dozes beside her. Phillip is sifting through his mound of shells. Sitting on his knees with his moppy brown hair blowing in the breeze, he inspects each one with the bottomless concentration of a master jeweler. It's a quality that Brianna has always admired in her younger brother, how devotedly he approaches his interests. When it comes to more routine obligations like school, he has a harder time focusing, but then who really *wants* to focus on the right things? Watching him now, she can't help feeling a stab of envy: with the possible exception of Jump, she can't recall ever investing in anything with such passion.

2.

She met Jump last winter through her friend Brooke, who had worked with him at Ben & Jerry's for three months before he just decided not to go in anymore. A couple times a week the girls would go over to his place to get stoned and watch campy horror movies from his extensive collection. *Hollywood Chainsaw Hookers. Chopping Mall. I Was A Teenage Werewolf.* He was heartbreakingly gorgeous, tall and slender with coffee-colored skin and eyes so powder blue they were almost translucent. Even his smell was sexy, a body spray-and-cigarette musk that made Brianna feel like her head might explode with desire.

But still: *nineteen.* Practically a man already. He understood things about the world, important things, like, say, how 9/11 had to have been an inside job because if you studied the YouTube videos like he had, you could see the explosions from the demolition charges. To hear him hold forth on the subject like a philosopher was always exhilarating, and so Brianna kept her affections to herself, letting them fester in her gut like a parasite, until one night after a party at Brooke's when she and Jump found themselves alone on a sofa in the basement. Prior to him, she had been with only two other guys, pimple-faced boys from school whom she regarded with the dull tolerance of a convenience store clerk. With them, all her insecurities about her body were canceled out by her repulsion at the mechanics of the whole thing—all that frantic, sweaty groping. With Jump, however, she'd been poignantly aware that she was naked. And she actually *wanted* his judgment, that was the weird thing. She wanted him to like her, yes, but she also wanted to prove to herself that she was someone worthy of being judged.

With this in mind, it's easy to see how he might have felt ambushed last week when she walked into his grungy studio apartment unannounced and, like an idiot, blurted, "So, I'm late."

He was seated on his leather loveseat packing his ceramic Buddha bong, authentic Sri Lankan. For a moment he gave her a confused scowl, until comprehension finally sank in. "Wait, you mean late, like, with your period?"

"About two weeks now." Actually, it was three but she was playing it safe, mainly for his sake. Missing a week here or there wasn't unusual for her, but at three she figured it was time to bring him into the loop. Although maybe that wasn't the right word. Can you even have a loop with just two people?

He gawped at her like she'd just pulled a gun on him. "Well Christ, don't look at me. Who else have you been screwing?"

Without thinking, she grabbed an empty Sprite can from the counter and hurled it at him. It missed him by a good foot and a half, striking the wall with a clatter and then falling to the dingy carpet.

"Don't throw stuff at me!" he whined.

"Well, don't call me a slut!"

"I didn't call you a slut. I just asked if you—"

"I heard you! And no, there's nobody else, okay? Jesus!"

He took a breath. Scratched the back of his neck. "Is it maybe stress? I've heard that can, like, fuck up your cycles."

"I don't know. Could be."

"That's got to be it. I mean, with finals and everything, you know?"

"Yeah." Nodding, Brianna looked at the fraying laces of her Chuck Taylors and ran her ponytail through her fists. "That's probably all it is."

Jump chewed on the inside of his cheek for a few seconds. Setting the bong on the coffee table, he leaned back and crossed his arms thoughtfully across his chest; the sleeves of his t-shirt pulled back to reveal his well-defined biceps. "Because it's just—and I don't want to sound like a prick or whatever—but I *always* pull out. You know that."

3.

The next day the Copelands venture to an outlet mall a few miles from the hotel. While the rest of the family heads to the food court, Brianna sets off in search of a gift for Jump. It occurred to her this morning that this was the best way to smooth things over, a gift. Guys like gifts, that's what Brooke insists, so long as it's the right kind. Meaningful but also practical. Nothing too sentimental, they hate that.

The wallet display in the window of a leather shop catches Brianna's eye: three tiered bins, each of them heaped with discount billfolds, clutches, and card holders. Inside, the robust tang of oiled leather is thick enough to gag on. Classic rock blares from speakers in the top corners of the room, some grainy-throated singer wailing about highways and lost love. As Brianna is scanning the merchandise, the lone sales clerk wanders over to ask if she needs anything. Instinctively, she gives the woman a quick up-and-down. Dressed in factory-torn jeans and a fringed black vest, she has the woeful good looks of a former beauty queen, her thick crust of makeup cracking at the creases around her plump lips. What Brianna first perceives as a beer gut beneath her t-shirt she quickly realizes is in fact a pregnant belly.

"I'm looking for a wallet. For my boyfriend."

"Okay, well, what does he like?"

"I'm not sure."

"Does he wear a chain? We sell a lot of those to guys."

Brianna studies the swell of the woman's baby bump. She fusses with a hank of hair behind her ear. "He's not really into that."

"Alright, so something more traditional. Maybe just a regular bifold?" She plucks a dark brown wallet from the bin and holds it out to Brianna. Would Jump like this? Hard to say. He needs a new wallet, that's for certain—the organic hemp one he's carried for years has started to look like a clump of old bandages. But he likes his accessories to have *personality*, nothing mass-produced or corporate, which doesn't leave a lot of options.

Except, as Brianna pretends to examine the bifold, turning it over in her hand the way her mother might inspect a piece of fruit at the grocery store, it occurs to her with some embarrassment that for all she knows about Jump's dislikes, she knows almost nothing about what he *does* like.

She nods at the woman's baby bump. "Is that uncomfortable?"

The woman glances down at herself, shrugs. "Sometimes, I guess. Makes me pee a lot, mostly."

"What's it feel like?"

She angles her mouth in a curious little smirk. "It's weird. Kinda like you're in someone else's body. You feel sick a lot for no reason and your joints hurt like hell. But it's a good kind of hurt, like after a really intense workout, you know?"

No, Brianna doesn't know, but she nods anyway to appease the woman.

"You wanna feel?"

"I'm not sure."

"Here, she's moving."

Before Brianna can protest, the woman grabs her wrist and pulls her t-shirt up over her stomach and places her hand on it. The skin, taut and smooth, feels like a rubber suit of some sort. Something you might wear to explore the bottom of the ocean.

"Do you feel it?"

Brianna shakes her head, and the woman moves her hand to the other side of the bulge. "How about now?"

"No."

"Hm. I dunno. She's definitely moving around in there."

As she presses down into the woman's rigid skin, Brianna vaguely recalls feeling her mother's belly when she was pregnant with Phillip. She was fascinated by the notion that a person, even a partially developed one, could thrive in such a tiny space, and the sensation of her unborn brother pushing out from beneath the flesh was . . . well, is there even a word to describe it? *Otherworldly* perhaps? Here she was communicating with this soon-to-be-person who didn't even really exist yet. *He's reaching for me,* she thought. *He hasn't even been born yet, and he's reaching for me.*

"Ow, honey. Not so hard."

It's not until the woman wrenches her hand from her belly that Brianna realizes how firmly she's been bearing down on her stomach, her fingers digging in up to the knuckle.

"Sorry."

"It's fine. Sometimes it's hard to feel from the outside."

As the woman is pulling the hem of her t-shirt back down, Brianna catches a glimpse of the handprint she left in her skin, the ghostly blear of her fingers like a prehistoric cave painting. The woman offers that beauty pageant smile again, but it's different this time. Less certain. "Anyway, is that the one you want?"

It takes Brianna a second to realize that she's referring to the bifold wallet in her other hand. Now she looks over at the heap of wallets in the bins, the collection of brown hues like a mound of freshly turned dirt, and then down at the one she's holding as if wondering how it got there.

Dumbly, she nods and follows the woman over to the register to ring it up. "I hope he likes it," she chirps as she drops it in a bag. Brianna, mumbling her thanks, reluctantly takes the bag as though she's being handed a used tissue and exits the store into the busy atrium. As soon as she's out of sight of the woman, she tosses it into a trash can.

4.

Because Phillip rarely has the patience for dine-in restaurants, especially in unfamiliar environments like this one, dinner that night is at a seafood buffet on the downtown boardwalk. *OVER 167 ITEMS!* proclaims the giant smiling crab looming over the entrance. Brianna gorges herself on crabcakes and fried shrimp and stuffed clams and potato salad and mac and cheese and, for dessert, a shameful glob of Oreo pie. By the time the family ambles out of the restaurant she feels like she might puke, though she knows it's more than just the food. Part of it is her encounter with the saleswoman at the leather store, still resonating in her mind. Why couldn't she feel the baby move? *Sometimes it's hard to feel from the outside.* Obviously, this was intended to be reassuring, but that wasn't the way Brianna heard it. To her, it sounded like a warning.

They wander down the boardwalk past kitschy seafood dives, gift shops, and t-shirt booths. The air is rich with the aromas of fried foods and sunscreen. On the other side of the boardwalk are the reedy sand dunes of the beach, and beyond that the ocean. In the twilight, the water is the color of a fresh bruise and every wave on the horizon looks like a shark's fin. Brianna envisions legions of the creatures swarming beneath the surface like something from one of Jump's horror movies, patiently waiting for the next unsuspecting victim.

Phillip, strolling shoulder-to-shoulder with his parents to avoid bumping into strangers, makes a sudden beeline toward an old-fashioned arcade. Video games are one of his passions, especially the bloody first-person-shooters, the gorier the better. Brianna has never been able to reconcile this with his comprehensive list of phobias, but if there's one thing she's learned about the logic of autism, it's that emotions can often domino into one another with no transition: one second he'll be skittish and withdrawn, the next he's practically vibrating with excitement. Sometimes it's disorienting how effortlessly he can shift between gears. When he was a toddler, you could spend an hour calling his name, and he wouldn't so much as look at you. But if you got right down in front of him and met his eyes, his chubby face would light up with recognition, and he would smile as if to say *I've been waiting for you.*

"Hang on, bud," Ray calls. "No running off. You have to ask, remember?"

"Can I go in, please?"

"I bet if you ask your sister nicely, she'll take you."

"She doesn't want to go in."

"Got me there," Brianna replies, scrolling aimlessly through her newsfeed. She snaps a few shots of the water by itself and then a single selfie against the horizon, the tip of her tongue poised seductively on her teeth. A little something to snag Jump's attention.

"See?" says Phillip, rolling his eyes. He clenches and unclenches his fists, an anxious tic. "Told you."

To Brianna, Ray says, "Look, your mom wants to find a bathroom, okay? Just go in for a few minutes. You'll survive, I promise."

Brianna considers arguing, but acquiescing now might buy her some time to herself later.

And so with a reluctant groan, she ushers her brother into the jungle of machines, with its digital chorus of beeps and explosions. After a couple minutes of inspecting his options, Phillip settles on a hunting game that involves killing computerized forest animals with a rubber rifle. As he begins cramming quarters into the coin slot, Brianna steps away to give Jump another call. She squeezes herself into a small alcove between two adjacent rows of machines where the noise isn't too bad but she can still keep an eye on her brother.

Not surprisingly, it goes straight to voicemail. Brooke claims there's an art to leaving a voicemail for a guy. "You have to be straightforward but not clingy," she explained a couple weeks ago. This was during the girls' post-school drive to the edge of the county, where they could smoke without being spotted by anyone they knew (at sixteen, Brooke already has a conditional license and a hand-me-down Taurus from her mother). "It's all about sounding, like, decisive. Like you know exactly what you want."

"But what am I supposed to be deciding?"

She squinted at Brianna like the question didn't make any sense. "What does *that* matter?"

Before Brianna is able to leave a message, however, she spots a scrum of kids hovering around Phillip, four boys and two girls. Evidently, they're amused by his technique of holding the gun out with one hand instead of sighting it up the proper way. One of them, a black-haired kid in ankle-length shorts, reaches playfully for the weapon as if to offer instruction. Phillip jerks away and continues firing at the screen like nothing has happened. Whether his inability to recognize ridicule is a blessing or a curse, Brianna has never been able to decide, but in any event his reaction, or lack thereof, only seems to provoke Black Hair. The kid makes to grab the rifle again, over and over like a game, prompting sniggers from the rest of the group. He's trying to get a rise out Phillip. But Phillip doesn't *rise*, not like you would expect. Instead, he stifles his feelings for as long as possible until his mind can't take it anymore, and soon enough you've got yourself a meltdown like the one at the rec center pool.

Brianna, still watching like a voyeur as her brother passively endures the kids' teasing, knows she should step in, but for some reason she can't bring herself to creep out of her hiding spot. What she really wants is to shake Phillip by his shoulders and howl at him to just stand up for himself already. *Throw a punch!* she thinks. *Stop being such an easy fucking target!* The thought makes her queasy with shame, but she can't stop herself: why does *she* have to feel helpless on his behalf? Where is the kid who boldly reached for her while he was still in the womb, not even knowing what was out there?

One of the girls, a scrawny thing with eye shadow the color of barbecue sauce, says laughingly to Black Hair, "Nick, quit being an asshole." From her voice it's apparent that Phillip is nothing more than a minor impediment in their night of fun.

One last fake lunge for the gun and Black Hair gives up, bored. As the group staggers off, Brianna watches her little brother drop another handful of quarters into the game, calm as a monk, before he recommences killing the on-screen animals, and it's only then that she realizes that Jump's voicemail has been recording this whole time.

Half an hour later, after Ray has managed to corral a begrudging Phillip out of the arcade and the family has started moseying back toward the public parking deck, Brianna spots the clique of kids mulling around an ice cream stand. Black Hair is licking tendrils of melted chocolate off his wrist while Barbecue Girl shovels hunks of mint chocolate chip into her tiny mouth. All six of them are thumbing their phone screens with their free hands.

Maybe it's her lingering remorse for not having come to her brother's rescue that causes Brianna, lagging a couple yards behind her family, to stop a few feet from the group, studying them amidst the passing crowd. At first they look back in expectation, as though she might have something to offer them. And honestly, she wishes she did: despite the fact that they never even saw her in the arcade, and even though they don't deserve it, she feels compelled to offer some sort of explanation for her cowardice.

Instead, she waits a few beats until the scrutiny of her gaze begins to make them squirm, at which point she holds up her phone and takes a snapshot of the group. A few of them trade bewildered glances, as if this might be some kind of prank. Black Hair, his smudgy wrist still poised near his mouth, begins to say something, but Brianna is already tossing her hair over her shoulder and hurrying ahead to catch up with her family.

5.

By the sixth and final day of the trip, Brianna has had more than her fill of the beach—the loud, beer-bellied tourists, her frustrations with herself for not having gone with the much more sensible tankini set. Not that she's dying to go home, either. Too many things waiting for her back there, too much to confront. Stretched out on her towel, she scrolls through the hundred or so photos she's taken over the past week: moody ocean shots for the most part, a few quirky tourist traps like the life-sized King Kong at the Wax Museum. Then there's her portfolio of selfies, none of which has elicited a response from Jump like she'd hoped. Just looking at them now makes her feel foolish.

But it's the shot of the kids from the arcade that she keeps coming back to. Those six scowling faces glaring back at her like a kind of challenge, their open mouths smeared with ice cream. Something about the image, its belligerent frankness, perplexes her. It reminds her of the time that someone in Mr. Weintraub's Life Sciences class asked if it was true that sharks can smell a single drop of blood from a mile away. This was during the oceanography unit, and while Brianna doesn't recall what prompted the question she does recall how Mr. Weintraub, a jowly bear of a man who wore his contempt for his students like a suit of armor, sighed and flexed his jaw the way he did whenever his lectures got derailed. "That's a myth. Pretty much everything people know about sharks comes from the movies. Fear, ladies and gentlemen, can make folks believe all kinds of crap."

As far as Brianna is concerned, even if people like Mr. Weintraub are right, why would you want to take the chance? After all, doesn't she know better than most the dangers of pressing your luck?

Or at least this was her opinion at the beginning of the week. Now though, it dawns on her that Mr. Weintraub was only half right: maybe people *want* something to be afraid of. Otherwise, the whole notion of safety loses all meaning. Because what's more frightening, sharks in the water, or realizing once you've willed yourself into the ocean that the threat was just something you invented, and now here you are with not a goddamn thing to show for your fear?

And so perhaps this is why she climbs off her towel and pads down the wet sand, past her mother and Phillip futzing with his shells, past Ray who taunts her with the *Jaws* theme until Carol gives him a playful swat on the arm, out toward the lush whitecaps.

Shells slice into her feet as she wades out into the surf. Waves crash against her as if to compel her back to safety. When she's far enough out that she has to stand on her toes, she lies back and closes her eyes, resigned to the understanding that if there really are things to be afraid of, it's up to her to draw them out.

No tourist noise this far out, no corny steel drum music from the hotel pool. Just the water's gentle sloshing against her skin. She floats until her muscles throb and all she can hear is her own heartbeat in her ears. Nothing is coming for her, no bloodthirsty predators—hasn't part of her known this all along? Possibly. And yet another part of her, the same one that kept her from coming to Phillip's defense in the arcade, is still disappointed: isn't her blood worth the taking, too?

As if in response to this thought, something slick brushes against Brianna's calf, sending a searing bolt of pain up through her leg.

She thrashes in the water, back toward the beach, her leg throbbing with each frantic kick. Her mind is alight with images of mangled limbs and torn flesh and bloodied shark teeth. A massive swell rises up beneath her and sends her somersaulting through the waves, until finally it deposits her in the shallow surf like a toy it's grown bored with. Shakily, she comes to her feet and examines the damage to her calf, only to find that there is no gory horror movie wound, just a small C-shaped welt a couple inches long. It feels like a burn, like she's been branded. A jellyfish sting, she realizes as she begins high-stepping her way to the shore, relieved but also embarrassed by her overreaction. Just a goddamn jellyfish.

That's when she spots Phillip standing ankle-deep in the surf, gazing out at her.

Except, that can't be right, can it? No, it can't be her brother, the same boy who screamed himself sick at the rec center pool, the one she ditched in the arcade when he needed her. And yet, here he is, his pudgy belly peeking over the waistband of his swim trunks, watching her limp toward him. Watching and waiting. He'll pester her with questions for days to come, because that's the only way he knows to make sense of uncertainty—*Were you drowning? Why did you go in the water?*—but for now she's just grateful to see him standing there with his arm outstretched as if to welcome her back to shore, and so she reaches across the roiling waves that threaten to sweep her back out into nothingness, straining to touch her brother's fingertips.

Monsters

During the fall of his seventh-grade year, Mitchell Foster operated a small business on the playground of Trinity Middle School: for five dollars apiece, he would allow his classmates to kick him in the crotch. The idea had come to him earlier that year when Brian St. Clare, who sat behind him in homeroom and was fond of taping sloppy illustrations of penises onto his back, jokingly offered to give him a dollar if Mitchell allowed Brian to punch him in the face. "A whole dollar," Brian had teased. "Maybe you can use it to buy some deodorant." Mitchell had laughed off the offer, as he did most of Brian's insults, although some part of him was intrigued by the idea. He thought of the minister-slash-body builder who had come to the school the previous year to give a speech on the physical benefits of prayer, the one who had smashed a stack of boards to splinters with a single chop. "True strength isn't the ability to cause pain," the man had said, his gruff baritone booming through the gym PA system, "but to withstand it."

Within weeks Mitchell was making between fifteen and thirty dollars per recess period. It wasn't as much as he'd hoped—it turned out that most of his classmates were more interested in *watching* him take the kicks than actually delivering them—but at least Brian St. Clare had stopped taping penis sketches to his back, and anyway, as his dad might have said, money was money.

Ironically, very few of his fellow students knew how to land a proper kick. Most were too scared of hurting him to put the necessary effort into it, striking instead with the top arch of the foot instead of the toe, which as far as Mitchell was concerned, was the proper way to kick someone in the balls. Not that it made much difference; the double-layer ski mitten that he secretly stuffed down his underwear absorbed most of the impact, allowing him to withstand around five kicks per recess period. Each day, he would draft a different student to handle the money for him, promising him or her ten percent of that day's profits. The rest of his earnings he stashed in an envelope behind his dresser to be put toward a telescope he'd seen in *Science Life*; according to the ad, you could actually see the *surface* of Mars. Ever since his trip to Space Camp the previous year, he'd been obsessed with the planet. It was the mystery of it: a vast rugged wasteland close enough to taunt the imagination but just out of Earth's reach.

As his customer base expanded, Mitchell knew it was only a matter of time before the cluster of students in the gym alcove finally attracted the suspicions of Sister Rowland, the recess monitor, whose long, severe face and gaunt frame had earned her the nickname Lurch. But how could he stop? He was too enamored with the attention that the business brought him, even if it did sometimes leave him unable to move with more than a stiff waddle. People greeted him in the halls now, asked him how his balls were holding up lately. "Does it hurt?" they'd say with knotted looks of discomfort, as if just talking about it caused them pain.

"Kinda. Not really. I like the way it feels."

This wasn't true, but Mitchell needed them to believe that he was impervious, a tough guy. In reality, he was a stocky pan-faced boy with an endocrinal condition that caused him to sweat excessively and lent him the faint but constant aroma of dirty socks. Naturally, this made him unpopular, as did his habit of mouth-breathing while trying to focus in class. Over the past year, things had started speeding up, time seemed to be passing more quickly than it used to, making him feel cut off from his peers. Friends he'd had less than a year before were moving on to new cliques, adopting new personalities, becoming unfamiliar. His hope was that such a demonstration of fortitude might finally earn him their appreciation.

Plus, there was the issue of his father: an economics professor at a small college, he had been accused of sexual misconduct by a female grad student the previous semester. It hadn't taken long for most of Mitchell's classmates to find out about the scandal—many of their parents worked at the college—and so he figured that proving himself as a tough guy might help insulate him from some of the ridicule.

This was what was going through his mind the morning that Blake Jameson stepped forward out of the rabble of students and timidly handed over his five dollars. A transfer student who had started at Trinity a month earlier, Blake was lanky and trim with wavy blond hair that fell across his forehead in a kind of girlish fringe. Mitchell was aware of who he was but had never met him personally, and so there was no way he could have known that at his previous school Blake been a forward on the soccer team.

The kick was swift and elegant, the thick rubber bumper of Blake's sneaker connecting solidly enough with Mitchell's crotch to render the ski mitten useless. A crisp dagger of pain shot up through his midsection. The crowd issued a collective gasp and then fell silent as Mitchell collapsed into a ball onto the stiff grass, clutching himself between the legs, sputtering breathlessly, his scrotum swelling up with blood.

•

His left testicle had split nearly in half. It would have to be removed so that the dead tissue didn't spread. An *oriechtomy*, the doctor called this. "Don't worry, once it's healed, you won't notice any difference," he explained to all three Fosters. "You can do everything with one that you can with two. Kind of cool, huh?" Mitchell wanted to take comfort in this, but he knew that it wouldn't matter to the Brian St. Clares of the world. Word of his injury was guaranteed to spread, and the other kids would be ready to pounce as soon as he got back to school.

"I just don't understand," Mr. Foster said on the drive home from the hospital. Mitchell, seated in the middle of the back seat so that he could keep his legs spread, could tell from his father's flushed cheeks that he was trying to keep his anger under control. "Why would you do this to yourself? Charge people money to hurt you? Don't you have any self-respect?"

"I have self-respect," Mitchell replied groggily. He didn't see how self-respect had anything to do with it.

"I mean, is this some kind of cry for help? Do we need to take you to talk to someone?"

"Who?"

"A professional. A doctor. Someone who might know what this is all about. Because this, this is really unhealthy." Mr. Foster issued a heavy sigh. He was broad-shouldered with a stately gut and deep-set eyes that Mitchell imagined as having been jammed into his skull by a pair of fat, calloused thumbs. He had one meaty hand on the wheel, the other rubbing his forehead. "You know, I ought to make you put all that money toward your hospital bills."

In the rearview, his mother angled her mouth into a sympathetic smile.

The recovery would take several weeks, the first two of which Mitchell had been instructed to spend at home to minimize his mobility. Actually, other than the soreness in his abdomen and the jock strap he was required to wear, the ordeal wasn't all that bad. He spent most of his time on the living room sofa, watching movies with the special heating pad they had given him at the hospital folded up between his thighs. A couple times a day his father would emerge from his cluttered office, where he spent the majority of his days listening to NPR and gazing longingly out the window, to give him his pain meds. "How're you feeling?" he'd say stiffly.

"I'm okay."

"How's the swelling?"

"It's getting better."

"You need anything?"

"I don't think so."

"Want some more pillows?"

"I'm okay."

"Here, let me get you some more pillows."

It was clear that Mr. Foster was embarrassed by his son's poor judgment, but Mitchell had long gotten used to humiliating the man. Frankly, he seemed to have a talent for it, like at Mr. Foster's grad student cocktail party the previous spring. His father held the party at the end of every academic year. The students, dressed in crisp blazers and skirt sets, would stand around in small groups, clutching flutes of champagne like trophies and eagerly waiting for Mr. Foster, whom they appeared to regard as a celebrity, to drift their way and make small talk. Mitchell had spent most of the evening gobbling down handfuls of pigs-in-a-blanket from one of the chafers of hors d'oeuvres, only to find himself on the toilet around midnight doubled over with a cramp. Perhaps not surprisingly, he ended up clogging the toilet, at which point he went to get the plunger from the downstairs bathroom.

The partygoers had left hours earlier and the house was dark and silent. Dirty plates and glasses littered the kitchen counter. As Mitchell passed the back door, he heard voices from somewhere outside, a man's and a woman's. He recognized the man's voice as his father's, but the woman's he couldn't place. It wasn't his mother's; she had stumbled off to bed around the same time as him, unsteady and droopy-eyed from all the champagne.

Mitchell stepped out onto the patio. "Dad?"

From the decorative garden bench near the flowerbed off to the side of the patio, two figures sprang to their feet—Mr. Foster and one of the girls from the party, a petite blonde in a blue pencil skirt. The cardigan she had been wearing earlier that evening now hung over the back of the bench.

"Hey, pal," Mr. Foster said with uncharacteristic brightness, stepping out of the shadows onto the patio. "What's—what's going on?"

Instinctively, Mitchell's eyes went to the girl. She was smoothing down the front of her skirt with nervous, jerky strokes. He waited for his father to acknowledge her, but the man just stood there with his arms crossed anxiously over his chest, looking down at Mitchell with a wide-eyed smile, like they had been expecting him all along.

Mitchell motioned for his father to lean in close. "I clogged the toilet again," he whispered into his ear.

"What? I can't hear you."

"I clogged the toilet again."

"Ah, okay, well then . . . " Mr. Foster offered the girl a quick businesslike smile and then, placing his hand on the back of Mitchell's neck, steered him gently toward the back door. "I will take care of that. Why don't you wait for me here, and I will be right back." Stepping inside, he flipped on the kitchen light. "Just wait here, inside."

After his father had disappeared upstairs, Mitchell sat down at the table to wait, his stomach gurgling queasily. On the counter, the empty chafers, which had been left open, seemed to glare at him like a pair of lifeless eyes. He felt foolish for having come to his father about the toilet, though he didn't understand why. It was something about how eager he'd been to hustle him inside, away from the girl. As though she might be dangerous.

After a couple minutes, the back door opened, and the girl tiptoed inside. She must have assumed that Mitchell had gone back upstairs with his father because she looked surprised to see him. "Oh, hi there," she whispered, giving him the wide toothy grin of someone mugging for a camera. Her cardigan was back on, wrinkled and misbuttoned. "So, you're Dr. Foster's son, right? Your dad is seriously *always* talking about you."

•

Mitchell was watching some old sci-fi movie—an alien virus turns people into these large, flesh-hungry, spiderlike creatures—when, through the front window, he spotted Blake riding his bike up the driveway. His hair, so blond it looked bleached of all color, glimmered in the afternoon sun. The Jamesons, whose subdivision was only a few streets up from the Fosters', had made arrangements for Blake to come over to offer a proper apology (there had been some grumblings about taking the Jamesons to court over the medical expenses, but ultimately his parents had determined that Mitchell's having invited the kick wasn't likely to earn much sympathy from a judge). Hiding the heating pad beneath the cushions, Mitchell struggled up into a sitting position and draped his arm over the back of the sofa, affecting a look of casual disinterest.

Mr. Foster escorted Blake into the living room. "Hey," Blake said.

"Hey."

To Blake, Mr. Foster said with a note of admonishment, "He's very sore." Then, addressing both of them: "We don't always make good decisions, do we boys?" It wasn't the sort of question that needed an answer.

Blake stared at the floor. Mitchell glared at his father, willing him to shut up and leave.

For a few moments after Mr. Foster had skulked back down the hall, Blake hovered in the doorway, his hands buried in the pockets of his cargo shorts.

"Want to sit down?" Mitchell said.

"Okay." He took a seat in the armchair next to the couch. "My parents made me come here. They wanted me to tell you I'm sorry."

"It's okay."

"Does it hurt real bad?"

"Not really."

Blake nodded. "That's good. Man, when you fell down like that, I was like, *Holy crap, what did I do?*" He laughed unconvincingly, an uneasy twitter.

An awkward silence settled between them, and they shifted their attention to the movie, watching as the main character, a scientist, flailed around a laboratory, smashing into microscopes and racks of specimen jars, shrieking in agony as pincers sprouted from inside his mouth and two sets of bristly black legs, fully formed, burst from his sides.

After a couple minutes, Blake said, "Hey, so like, is it true?"

"What?"

"That they had to cut out your nut?"

"Yeah. But you can do everything with one that you can do with two, that's what the doctor said."

Blake lowered his head and put his hands over his eyes. "I didn't mean to," he said, more to himself it seemed, and after a few seconds Mitchell realized that he was crying. "Everybody else was doing it and I thought it would be fun or whatever. They said it didn't hurt. You, I mean. They said it didn't hurt you. Everybody knew about the mitten."

"They did?"

Blake wiped his nose with the back of his hand, trying to regain his composure. "Yeah, they did. They said it wouldn't hurt. I didn't mean for you to go in the hospital."

Mitchell stared at the back of Blake's bowed head. He glanced around the room as if in search of an explanation for what was happening. Something about Blake sitting there next to him crying seemed unnatural, a breach in logic. He was crying because of *him*,

Blake was, and while it made Mitchell feel bad for him, there was something gratifying about it, too, about knowing that he could elicit such a reaction.

"It's okay," Mitchell said in a near murmur. He ran the back of his arm across his sweaty forehead. "It was an accident."

They played a few rounds of *Wii Tennis*, Mitchell sitting spread-legged on the couch while Blake bounced back and forth across the rug, slinging the controller with a determined grimace. Mitchell kept stealing glances at Blake, both stunned and a little amused by how seriously he took the game, especially in light of his crying jag earlier. In fact, Blake appeared to have completely forgotten about the incident. Or maybe that was just the impression he wanted to give.

"Dammit!" he exclaimed after missing another of Mitchell's serves. "Something's wrong with this controller."

"We can play *Mario Kart* instead, if you want," Mitchell said. "It's easier."

"No, we're finishing this game," Blake replied, shaking out his wrists as though preparing for a strenuous workout. "It's just this stupid controller keeps messing me up."

When they'd grown bored with the game, they went upstairs into Mitchell's room. Mitchell broke out the science kit he had received for Christmas but never figured out how to use. Supposedly, you could mix a few chemicals together and create some kind of glow-in-the-dark goo, but after following the directions in the booklet the boys only managed to produce a rank yellowish broth.

"I don't think we did it right," Mitchell noted, staring down into the container of goop.

"This crap stinks, dude," Blake said.

While Mitchell studied the instruction booklet to see where they'd gone wrong, Blake ambled about the room, inspecting the complicated sketches taped to the walls—prototypes of Martian exploration vehicles, Mitchell explained. Blake picked up the copy of *Science Life* from the desk, crinkled from so much use and already opened to the telescope ad.

When Mitchell saw him looking at the magazine, he said "I'm going to buy that telescope."

Blake turned the ad to the side, held the magazine close to his face to examine the illustration of a wide-eyed boy peering through the telescope, smiling. "Why?"

"Because," Mitchell said as if the reasons were obvious, "you can, like, actually see Mars."

"Seriously?"

"That's what it says, see?"

"Huh." For a moment Blake appeared puzzled. "But there's nothing there on Mars. Just rocks and stuff."

"So?"

"So, then, like, what's there to see?

"I don't know," Mitchell said, looking at the floor and shrugging. "I just think it's cool. It's something different."

Blake pursed his lips thoughtfully. He dropped the magazine back on the desk. "If you say so." He went over to the corner of the room and sunk down into the red beanbag chair. In a conspiratorial whisper, he said, "Hey, can I ask you something?"

"Sure," Mitchell said.

"What happened with your dad?"

Mitchell glanced at the floor. He could tell from Blake's tone that it was an honest question, but the bluntness of the phrasing rattled him. *What happened with your dad?* Like they were gossiping about a classmate.

"My dad?"

"Yeah."

"Why?"

Blake shrugged. "I was just wondering."

Mitchell fumbled inattentively with one of the clear glass vials. "Some girl said he, like, made her do stuff. So she could pass his class."

"What stuff?"

"I don't know. Sex and stuff, I think. She said he told her he'd make her lose her scholarship if she didn't do it."

As a matter of fact, Mitchell knew very little about the scandal other than what his mother had divulged one evening a few glasses into her nightly wine regimen, which was that even really smart men like Duncan Foster sometimes made really stupid decisions. "He's still a child in a lot of ways," she'd said, speaking to no one in particular. "Some mid-life crisis thing maybe, I'm not sure." Mitchell had wanted to ask her what this meant, what kind of stupid decisions she was talking about, but the icy distance in her voice told him it was best to just leave it alone.

"You think it's true?" Blake said.

"No way." He threw Blake a challenging look and then caught himself and shifted his eyes back down to the vial. "He says she's just mad because she was going to fail."

"A couple of people said he might go to jail."

"Who said that?"

"Just kids at school." Hastily, he added, "But they're all dumb, right?"

Mitchell surveyed the scattering of vials and beakers and specimen jars. He had forgotten which step he was on in the instruction booklet.

"Yeah," he said quietly. "They don't know anything."

•

A few days later, Mitchell returned to school. In homeroom, Laura Clancy asked if he could still get a boner, and if so could he still have kids. Brian St. Clare suggested he bury the ruptured testicle to see if maybe he could grow a whole new set of balls. Mitchell, having prepared himself for such a reception, chuckled good-naturedly at the barbs, reminding himself that within a few days they'd wear the issue out and forget all about him again.

What he hadn't braced himself for was the rise of Blake's popularity in the wake of the accident. He discovered this during lunch when he spotted Blake playing basketball with Tyler Hauser and a few other boys. Tyler, who was rumored to have once dunked so hard on one of the goals at the Emmanuel Baptist rec center that the rim had snapped clean off, spearheaded most of the lunchtime games, which were understood to be invite-only.

Strange then for Blake to be playing, especially considering that no one had even known his name up until two weeks earlier.

Even stranger, Mitchell considered as he eased himself onto one of the cold metal benches to watch the game, a gesture of support for his friend, was how terrible Blake was. Each time the ball found its way into his hands, he would immediately lob it toward the basket, and invariably each time it would glance off the backboard and into the hands of someone from the other team. On the few occasions that he did pass the ball, it was almost always intercepted. However, if Blake had any idea how unskilled he was, he didn't let on; no doubt this had to do with the friendly back slaps that Tyler would give him each time he missed a shot or turned over the ball, telling him not to worry about it, it was no big deal.

That afternoon Mitchell approached Blake in the hallway by his locker. "Hey," he said, giving him a friendly nudge in the shoulder.

Blake peered warily around the crowded hall. "Hey."

"What class are you going to?"

"Civics."

"Do you want to come over and play Wii this afternoon?"

Blake scowled. "Can't."

"How come?"

"Got stuff to do."

Mitchell could feel a blush working up through his neck and face. He wasn't sure what to make of the flatness in Blake's tone.

"Then can you come over tomorrow?"

"I dunno. I'm supposed to go over to Tyler's."

"Well, then is there another time that you want to play Wii?"

Blake made a face. "Not sure. Don't be such a clinger."

"I'm not a clinger."

"Whatever," Blake chuckled, shutting his locker with a loud clang and strutting off down the hall. Mitchell watched him go, listening to his shoes squeak rhythmically on the floor.

•

In the movie Mitchell had watched with Blake, the scientist's wife had come looking for him at the lab after he hadn't been home in a couple days. When she'd found him cowering in a dark corner, a hulking mass of arachnid appendages, unrecognizable as the man she loved, she had shrieked in horror. But then she'd spotted his wedding band, which had inexplicably remained on his gnarled claw after his transformation, and in a shaky voice had said, "John, is that you?" Taking a step forward, she reached out and timidly touched one of his pincers, running the tips of her fingers over the stiff tiny hairs. The scientist recoiled in shame. The wife said, "Oh my god, it *is* you!"

Mitchell thought about the scene later that night as he undressed for bed. Change was easy, he considered, but changing *back*, returning to a previous state—well, that was something else entirely, wasn't it? Standing before the full-length mirror on his closet door, he ruefully examined the pudgy folds and curves of his own body, the sickly white hue of his skin, like something subterranean, unevolved. He looked at the scar running down the middle of his scrotum like a seam, and he wondered how much of yourself you had to lose before you became something else altogether. Before you became a monster.

•

The next day at lunch, Mitchell reclaimed his seat on the bench to watch the basketball game. Blake glanced over at him as he sat down but otherwise didn't acknowledge him. Once again, he watched Blake run through parade of air balls and missed layups, and once again Tyler Hauser offered up his toady praise after each one. People should know where they belong, and Blake didn't belong on the court. And yet, there he was, lobbing a three-pointer from the right edge of the key, while Mitchell could only watch from the bench.

The ball banked against the rim and went sailing over the boys' heads, out into the grass, coming to rest just a few feet from Mitchell. "Throw it here!" one of the boys shouted. Mitchell picked it up and surveyed the boys' sweaty faces. There was Blake, hands on his hips, panting heavily. He was watching Mitchell with the same blank stare he had given him in the hall the day before.

"Throw it!"

Mitchell wrapped his arms around the ball, clutching it to his belly.

Tyler said, "Blake, tell your boyfriend to give us the ball."

"Shut up," Blake hissed. "He's not my boyfriend." He slumped across the court toward Mitchell.

He stopped a couple feet from him, and the two of them held each other's gaze. The other boys hovered a few feet behind. "Give us the ball." Blake said.

"No."

"Why?"

"Because."

"Because what?"

"Because you're being mean." Mitchell hated how whiny he sounded, like a little kid, but he couldn't help it. How could someone do an about-face so easily? Just a few days earlier Blake had cried in front of him. He'd actually *cried*. Shouldn't that have ratified their relationship somehow?

"You're being a baby. Give us the ball." Blake was trying to sound cold, defiant, but Mitchell could detect a faint tremor in his voice.

"*You're* the baby. You cried at my house." To the other boys, he yelled, "He cried! At my house!"

Blake took a step forward, close enough so that Mitchell could smell his sweat. "Shut up."

"You can't come over to my house anymore!"

"Like I even care."

"And you can't look at my telescope when I get it, either! And you can't be my friend anymore!"

"I was never your friend, faggot." Blake threw the other boys a quick look as if to make sure he was handling the situation appropriately. Tyler gave an approving snigger, prompting the others to do the same. Blake leaned in close to Mitchell, a cruel grin lingering at the corners of his mouth. "At least my dad's not a sick perv."

At first, it didn't even register with Mitchell that the ball had left his hands, not until he heard the airy *poing* of it connecting with Blake's thin, delicate nose and then rolling off into the grass. Blake yelped and flailed backward, cupping his nose as thick rivulets of blood seeped out from between his fingers, staining the front of his green polo a grisly brown.

For a few moments, everybody gaped silently at Blake, including Mitchell. He tried to speak, not entirely sure of what he was going to say.

"I didn't—"

But before he could finish the thought, Blake was on him a fury of slaps and punches. He wrestled him backward onto the bench. Mitchell struggled as best he could, but the strain in his unhealed groin made it difficult. It wasn't until he felt other hands pinning him down that he realized the other boys had encircled them, their flushed faces now crowding his field of vision, suffocating him. With violent agility, Blake crawled on top of him and clawed wildly at his face and hair, his fingernails tearing tiny tracks of skin from Mitchell's forehead.

"Make him show his nut!" someone shouted.

"It's probably all fucked up!"

"Let's see it!"

Now Mitchell began to thrash his legs as hard as he could, ignoring the hot needling pain between his legs, trying to wriggle away before Blake had a chance to unbuckle his belt, but the hands, they kept multiplying somehow, holding him down and pulling greedily at his clothing, the boys' faces only inches from his, he was pinned to the cold gray metal and they were going to pull his pants off, right there on the playground, he could feel the fabric sliding down his legs in jerky increments, past his knees and then his ankles, and all he wanted was to not cry, *not* cry, not here in front of these boys but no, too late, he was already bawling.

Then, all at once, the hands were gone, and he opened his eyes to see Sister Rowland looming over the group of boys, her bony face warped into an expression of slack-jawed horror at the scene. The other boys, frozen in place, peered back up at her like thieves caught in the act. To Blake, who was still clutching the legs of Mitchell's jeans—they had gotten hung up on his ankles—she said through gritted teeth, "Son, I think you better give those back."

•

His father was called to the school to pick him up. The two of them were silent for most of the drive home, Mr. Foster staring straight ahead, gripping the wheel with both white-knuckled hands. Mitchell leaned his head against the window, his eyes still raw and moist from crying. Outside, the cold wind battered the trees and sent trash skittering along the sidewalks.

"I'm calling Wes when we get home," Mr. Foster said as they pulled up at a red light. Wes was his lawyer and close friend of the family. "I want you to tell him what they did."

"I don't want to."

Closing his eyes, he sighed. "I know you don't. But you can't keep letting people treat you this way. You have to stand up for yourself."

Mitchell looked at his father out of the corner of his eye and then back out the window. "What did you do?"

His father threw him a puzzled scowl.

"What are you talking about?"

"At work. People say you did something. With some girl. They say you might go to jail."

Mr. Foster grimaced as if the question pained him physically. "I'm not going to jail."

"So then, what happened?"

"Look, you don't need to worry about it, okay?" His voice cracked on the last syllable in a way that made him sound tired, worn down— and in fact Mitchell was struck by how much older the man looked in that moment, his eyes underscored by deep shadowy lines, his broad shoulders drooping. He felt a pang of pity for him. "It's way more complicated than whatever these people are saying."

"How? How is it more complicated?"

"It's hard to explain."

"Tell me."

"Mitchell, I don't—"

"*Tell me!*"

The intensity in his voice made his father flinch. Where this outburst had come from, he didn't know, although he did know that it was about more than just Blake or what had happened on the playground. This was something less tangible, something that only now he realized had been building up inside of him for some time. For whatever reason, the image of the boy in the telescope ad popped into his head, and suddenly Mitchell wished that he could shake the kid by his stupid shoulders and scream at him that there was nothing up there worth seeking out, no escape, only the tantalizing promise of worlds he could never reach. At that moment, he hated the kid, deeply and viscerally enough to make his muscles ache, and it occurred to him that maybe on some level he had always hated him, just a little, because what did anyone really expect to find up there? *Just because something is far away,* he wanted to tell the kid, *that doesn't mean it's worth reaching.*

Mr. Foster shifted his gaze back out the windshield, his mouth hanging open slightly, like he was working through some complex problem in his head. Mitchell watched him, waiting for a response, until finally it became clear that he wasn't going to get one.

The light turned green, but before his father could press the accelerator Mitchell burst out of the car and took off down the street, tottering as fast as the excruciating soreness between his legs would allow. Behind him he could hear his father calling after him, his shouting barely audible above the car horns willing him to go before the light turned red again, but Mitchell didn't turn around. All he could do was keep moving in the opposite direction, past the line of stalled traffic, ignoring the confounded stares of the drivers wondering where he was going, what he was running away from.

The Fence

The trailer is a shabby doublewide the color of a coffee stain, nestled amidst the weeds at the top of the hill like a dozing animal. A vinyl awning sags over the door, which opens to a set of warped wooden stairs. Beyond it, the land slopes down a hundred yards or so toward the highway. That's where the kid was killed.

"The mom was in another room," Emmitt explains to Holt on the twenty-minute drive from Christiansburg into the circuitous network of mountain backroads. "Kid was autistic, something. Wandered down to the road, got squashed by a semi. Driver went nuts. They got him in the hospital over in Augusta."

In order to pacify the horrified neighbors, the city stepped in and determined that there should have been a fence surrounding the property to begin with, an overlooked county statute. And so now Emmitt pulls the large New River Valley Fences truck up the winding graveled drive, the trailer full of digging gear clanking along behind them, and then around the base of the hill so that he and Holt can install fifteen hundred feet of rail fence.

The morning is hot and dry, no clouds overhead, only the scorching August sun beating down on their arms and necks as Holt unloads the auger and posthole diggers and shovels and lumber, while Emmitt tromps off with his measuring wheel. The knee-high grass, still damp with dew, brushes against Holt's bare legs as he works. He got the job through his PO, who went to high school with Emmitt, following his release from Blue Ridge State Correctional four months earlier. The ad hoc interview took place at the rented stand-alone garage where Emmitt houses the truck and trailer. The place resembled a hardware store that had been sacked by a tornado, oil and grease-coated workbenches cluttered with tools, stacks of unused lumber and bags of Quickrete piled haphazardly against the corrugated metal walls. Spools of hurricane fence propped up in various corners.

"Way I see it, don't matter you've been in jail, so long as you're willing to work and don't cause me no problems," Emmitt told Holt in his husky baritone. "Had my son-in-law working with me for a while, but the boy couldn't hardly swing a hammer, was so stoned most of the time. That ain't how I run a business, you understand?"

"Yes, sir."

"You use drugs, son?"

"No, sir."

"I'm talking anything here, even a little weed."

"I don't."

The man nodded. He was resting his brawny arms on the top of the rusted tailgate. Holt put him somewhere around three-hundred pounds, a walrus of a man, with skin as dark as fresh asphalt. "Good. You drink?"

At this Holt paused. Technically speaking, he hadn't had a drop of anything since before being locked up. But like they were always saying at the AA meetings he'd been required to attend in prison, getting sober only means you stop drinking, it doesn't mean you stop being a drunk. The meeting moderator had been a high school geography teacher for twenty-two years until he'd driven his truck through the front of a Starbucks, and he was full of clever sayings like this. Another one that stuck with Holt was, *We are capable of change, though it's usually not the kind of change we'd like.*

And so finally Holt cleared his throat and looked at Emmitt and said, "Not anymore, no."

Emmitt's hooded eyes lingered on him for a moment, and in that silence Holt suspected that the man could see him for what he truly was: a loser, a wino criminal whose fiancé didn't want anything to do with him anymore, whose would-be stepdaughter would only ever know him as the man responsible for almost killing her.

But then Emmitt finally nodded to himself. "Good deal. I'll pick you up Monday morning at seven. Be outside."

Now Holt maneuvers the broad spiral blade of the auger through stubborn pockets of shale in the earth so that Emmitt can plant the posts. The powerhead bucks violently in his hands, making his entire body quake. By the time the sun is at its peak, his t-shirt is soaked through with sweat, clinging to his lean frame. As he works he keeps an eye on the doublewide at the top of the hill, hoping to catch a glimpse of the kid's mother. He wants to know what it does to you, losing a kid like that. But other than the battered red Pontiac in the driveway, the place is lifeless, the blinds drawn like the eyelids of a corpse.

Before being sent to prison, Holt was a grill cook at the American Buffet in Christiansburg. This was back when he was living with Charmaine and Kaylee in Charmaine's blocky little foursquare near the train depot. One afternoon he showed up to work to find his manager trashing the closet-sized office with an industrial ladle. Apparently, the corporate office had decided that their branch's numbers were too low—the restaurant was located in a failing strip mall where the only traffic seemed to be the teenagers who would show up in their jacked-up trucks at night to smoke cigarettes and blare their stereos until the cops arrived—and had shut the place down, effective immediately.

"So, what's that mean?" Holt asked the man.

The manager paused his bashing of the printer. He adjusted his red checked tie. Beads of sweat clustered in his scanty mustache. "Means we're out of a job."

"But they can't do that, can they? Without telling us?"

"They already did, amigo." He brought the ladle down on the paper tray, snapping it off with a fat crack.

Back at the house, Holt went through a six-pack in half an hour, downing the beers in only a few gulps apiece. What was he supposed to do now? File for unemployment most likely. Go stand in line at the job center downtown alongside all the other deadbeats with their sob stories. Not that he was in any position to judge. With no high school diploma and no technical skills, he'd been lucky to have a job at all.

When Charmaine got home from the salon, having picked up Kaylee at daycare, she found Holt slumped in the Lay-Z-Boy in front of the warbling television, his knuckles bruised and bloodied from the hole he'd punched through the wall in the wood paneled hallway. He hadn't meant to do it, not really. He'd just needed to put his fist somewhere, and the wall had seemed as good a place as any.

"Oh, this is great!" she howled. "This is *exactly* what I wanted to come home to!" Her midsection pooched over the waistband of her skinny jeans, too skinny for her chunky figure. Flaxen-colored roots shone through her dyed black hair.

Holt tried to explain to her about the restaurant's closing, but as far as Charmaine was concerned he had no one but himself to blame for his misfortunes. Before the American Buffet there was the drywall job, which he'd held for a year until the owner of the company retired to Florida to be near his grandkids, and before that the house painting gig that he'd had for six months until the housing market drop, and before that a host of other jobs that had lasted several months at a stretch before the powers that be determined Holt was no longer essential. To Charmaine, the solution was simple—Holt needed to get his GED, maybe enroll in the community college downtown. He needed real skills, not just the use of his hands. A *job*, she claimed, wasn't the same as a *career*. After all, there was Kaylee to think about, now four years old, and what if they ended up having more kids? A day laborer gig just wasn't going to cut it—time for him to start thinking ahead.

Holt didn't bother pointing out that he provided for Charmaine and Kaylee more than Charmaine's ex ever had, an ATV salesman who had refused to have anything to do with the pregnancy. Nor did he point out that he—Holt—was the one who had taught the girl to count to a hundred and had gotten her over her fear of the monster-infested closet and had even turned the spare change jug in the bedroom into a college fund. If that wasn't thinking ahead, then what was? Instead, he hefted himself out of the chair and stumbled to the door, just as Kaylee began bawling, her plump face folding in on itself like a hand curling into a fist, her customary response to their fighting. Ordinarily, he might have swept her up in his arms, twirled her around the room to get her giggling, but he didn't have it in him to be reasonable. Better to go grab a drink at the Cellar, wait for all of them to cool down.

Charmaine grabbed angrily at him as he crossed the room, her voice rising in pitch, but he swatted her hand off like a pesky insect, not even turning his head to look at her. As he reached the door he felt her grip his wrist with a sudden ferocity, her fingernails digging into his skin. Had his better judgment not been superseded by his booze-fueled temper, he probably would have been able to tell that it was Kaylee's hand, not Charmaine's. But as it was, he was too slow to stop himself from jerking his arm backward to free his hand, catching her under the chin with the back of his wrist and slamming her into a bookcase, her tiny head connecting against the corner with a hideous crunch. Like a beetle crushed beneath a boot. She collapsed face-first on the floor, blood blackening her fine blonde hair.

Charmaine let out an animal shriek and fell to the floor beside her, hauling the girl up into her lap and patting her cheeks to rouse her back to consciousness. "Come on, baby," she sobbed, "just open your eyes! Open your eyes for mama!" After a few seconds, Haylee's eyelids creaked open and Holt, who'd been standing motionless in the doorway, let out a long quivery breath.

It wasn't until much later, after the hospital and then the holding cell at the police station, that he would find out he had fractured her skull. That she hadn't slipped into a coma was nothing short of a miracle, according to the doctor. The judge, notoriously unsympathetic toward domestic abusers, was unmoved by Holt's plea that the whole thing had been one big accident and decided instead to make an example of him: a year in prison. Holt's publicly-appointed lawyer, a dumpy woman who carried pictures of her three Boston terriers in her wallet the way other people carry pictures of their kids, assured him that he could be out in five, maybe six months if he played his cards right.

"I've never cared much for cards," Holt responded dryly as the bailiff came to escort him back to his cell.

"Now's a good time to learn," the woman rejoined.

Drilling through the rocky earth proves to be more difficult than either Emmitt or Holt expected, and it ends up taking most of the week to plant the hundred and fifty posts. But Holt doesn't mind the work. It's good to be out in the sizzling sun, building something with his hands, his skin becoming tanned and his muscles thickening. Each day they work from seven-thirty until noon, at which point they break for half an hour to wolf down their sack lunches in the truck cab, Emmitt blasting the AC and listening to sports radio. After that it's back to work until four, by which point the sweat on their skins has dried to a tacky salt rime. By the end of each day, Holt feels like a prize fighter emerging victorious after a brutally prolonged match.

At the base of the hill is a windbreak of scrub pine insulating the property from the highway, where they go if they have to take a leak and where the whooshing sound of traffic from the highway on the opposite side blasts through like hurricane winds. Every time he's down there,

Holt can't help thinking about the dead kid. He must have tromped through these very trees on his way down to the road. What was he hoping to find? If his years with Kaylee have taught him anything, it's that kids' curiosity is a powerful and sometimes dangerous thing: it needs an outlet the same way the aimless rage of the men in Blue Ridge State Correctional needed one in their their free weights and cigarettes and board games. Without one what else is there to buffer you against the world?

This is what he's thinking on the afternoon that, standing in the chamber of trees, he hears voices coming from the other side, a man's and a woman's. The sound of the traffic drowns out the words, but he can tell from the shrillness of their tones that they're arguing. He shoulders his way through the pines, clouds of brambles scratching his shins and tugging at his clothes, before he emerges onto the graveled shoulder of the road. A few yards away is a battered black Tercel with a flat back passenger's side tire, the car canted to the side. A man is hunkered down fumbling with a scissor jack. He wears baggy shorts that hang down low enough to expose his lime green boxers and a long blue tank top that draws attention to his sinewy biceps, busy with cheap-looking tattoos. Holt can't make out the face of the woman in the passenger's seat, but he can hear her shouting something indecipherable at the man through the rolled down window. "Well, then you get your smart ass out here and do it!" he fires back as he cranks the handle. The woman rattles off something else, and the man barks, "I *am* twisting it! Goddammit, Darcy, would you let me work?"

Holt inches toward the stalled vehicle, his body buffeted by the airstream of the traffic to his left. "Need some help?" he calls out.

Flinching, the man springs to his feet. "Shit, dude, where'd you come from?"

"Doing some work up here." Holt gestures in the direction of the hill beyond the curtain of trees behind him. As he gets closer to the vehicle, the woman cranes around the headrest to look at him. She's a bottle redhead with a big nose and closely-set eyes and acne-scarred cheeks. In the backseat he notices a pair of boys probably no older than Kaylee. They have the woman's broad forehead and harshly-contoured face, chins like blades.

"Think I'm alright," the man says, twitching his fingers at his sides. "Must have run over a nail or something. I already got the donut on, just gotta tighten the nuts."

Standing only a few feet from the man now, Holt takes in his raw, watery eyes and the droop at the corners of his mouth, the slight waver in his posture. You go to enough meetings, you learn to recognize when someone is wasted. He can hear it in the man's voice, the edges of his words bleared like wet ink.

"Want me to call somebody?" he asks.

"No, I'm good. Thanks."

"Maybe you ought to let her drive."

"Hey, man," the fellow says with a note of annoyance, squaring back his shoulders, "I said we're good, alright? Why don't you go on back now, lemme fix this tire."

But Holt takes another step forward. He's thinking about the sharp clack of Kaylee's teeth as his arm connected with her jaw. "Just seems like you're not in the best condition to drive."

"Motherfucker, my *condition* ain't none of your business."

"What's he want?" the woman yells from inside the car.

"Nothing," the man replies.

"Does *he* know how to use the jack?"

"Darcy, I swear to god!"

"You okay to drive?" Holt calls over to her.

"Hey!" the man caws. "You got nothing to say to her, you hear me?"

He gives Holt's shoulder a firm poke that makes him stagger back a step, and before he can stop himself Holt shoves the man, a prison yard reflex, although it's about like trying to move an oak tree. He has an instant to realize the stupidity of what he's done before the fellow's fist crashes into the side of his face, sending him sprawling on the ground. Gravel slices his elbows and the back of his head, his face screeching in pain from the blow.

The man stands over Holt, the sun casting jagged shapes across his face. Thick snakelike cords bulge in his neck and forearms.

"Get up, see what happens, asshole," he growls.

Clutching his throbbing jaw, Holt glances from him to the kids in the backseat, who are watching the spectacle over the headrests with the beseeching expressions of hostages, open-mouthed and grubby-faced. The woman, too, is still eyeballing him from the open window, deciding whose side to take in the squabble. It's one of those tip-the-scale moments that he's come to know well, when any decision you make is bound to damn you in some way. A couple years ago he might have scrabbled to his feet and charged the guy, fists flailing. Maybe he would have gotten his ass kicked, but a man has to stand up for himself if he wants to command any respect. Or at least that was what he used to believe, back before being locked away. But if there's one thing he's picked up over the past year, it's that the right thing to do isn't always the responsible thing to do. Being a coward, he figures, is better than being busted back to Blue Ridge State Correctional for scrapping with a stranger.

And so, finally, Holt lifts his bloodied palms in surrender.

"Good decision," the man grunts. He continues staring down at him for another few seconds, his fists still poised at his side, before turning back to the car.

From the cigarette butt-strewn ground, Holt, still too dizzy to stand, watches him tighten the lug nuts and cram the flat tire in the hatchback, tossing the jack and the handle in on top of it with a clank. "You oughtta learn to mind your own business," he says as he stuffs his bulky body into the driver's seat. Holt can see the boys still peering at him as the vehicle lurches back onto the busy highway, the brakes whining, and then rumbles away.

That night Holt calls Charmaine. Legally, he isn't supposed to have any contact with her, but his altercation with the man has shaken something loose in him, and suddenly summoning the wrath of her lawyer seems like a risk worth taking. It's close to nine; by now she'll have a couple rum-and-Cokes in her, which means she might be more amenable to talking. His plan is to blindside her with the speech he concocted about mistakes and forgiveness and the importance of a male authority figure in a child's life. But when he hears her pick up, everything he planned to say scatters from his mind.

"What do you want, Holt?"

"Please don't hang up," he sputters.

"You're not supposed to be calling here."

"I was just hoping we could talk."

She sighs. "Nothing to talk about."

"How's things at the salon?"

"Didn't you hear me? We're not doing this."

Holt's apartment is a stale studio on the second floor of a boxy brick tenement, with a single closet and a rusted half-stove and a modest balcony onto which he now steps, lighting up a cigarette. The first drag makes his jaw ache. His fingers drift up to the fleshy knot near the angle of the bone. "How's Kaylee?"

Charmaine chokes out a humorless laugh. "I'll tell you how she is. She's got a big ugly scar on the back of her head, and she gets headaches when it rains. Does that answer your question?"

"Can I talk to her?"

"Are you out of your mind? Of course you can't talk to her. She's already in bed, anyway."

"She ever ask about me?"

"We're seriously not having this conversation."

Holt sucks deeply on the smoke, wincing at the flash of pain. "Goddammit, Charmaine, you know that girls who grow up without their fathers always turn out to be fucked up."

"You're not her father, Holt," she fires back. "Don't call us again, you understand? Or else you're gonna be in a world of shit."

Before he can respond, she clicks off. For a few moments, Holt stares at the phone in his hand, willing her to call him back, tell him the whole thing was a big misunderstanding. When that doesn't happen, he whips the thing across the room. It strikes the wall by the counter, leaving a dent in the drywall before clattering onto the cheap tile. When he picks it up he sees that the screen is spider-webbed with cracks, permanently frozen on the *CALL ENDED* notification.

The idea of spending one more night alone in the cramped apartment, chainsmoking to stanch the alcohol cravings, makes him think he might lose his mind, and so he decides to walk down the road to the 711 for a burrito. Having had his driver's license revoked, Holt's only occasion to leave the place, other than work and going for groceries, is the one day a week his sponsor picks him up for his court-mandated meetings. Beyond that, it's not much different than being in prison, the crippling loneliness, the insufferable boredom. He shuffles along the littered shoulder of the road, past the vacant machine shops and the squalid paper mill that lends the air a flatulent odor. A squadron of bats flits about the lighted industrial spires, gobbling up insects. He thinks about that night in the hospital, sitting in one of the waiting room's molded plastic chairs with his head dangling between his shoulders, looking up to see the two cops approaching, their faces set into looks of stony accusation. He recalls his first night in prison, his cellmate, a monstrous fellow everyone called Train, waking him shortly after lights out with a series of expert blows to the back of his head—a standard punishment among the inmates for laying hands on a kid—making Holt's eyes feel like they might pop right out of his skull. And Kaylee, he thinks about her too, her clean powdery little girl scent, how he never got a chance to apologize to her. To explain.

Up ahead is the store, the fluorescents over the door flickering unevenly, but his attention is drawn instead to the bar on the opposite side of the road. He's passed it hundreds of times but has never paid much attention to it, a dun-colored brick cube with bars on the door, the windows blacked out and adorned with blinking beer signs. This, he understands now as he finds himself migrating across the road, was the reason he left the apartment.

A nervous film of sweat breaks out on his forehead and the back of his neck as soon as he steps inside, as though the temperature has abruptly spiked. The place is muggy with decades of smoke and beer vapor, the nicotine-yellowed walls plastered with outdated ads, their colors bleached to a palette of dull greens and greys. A trio of burly men in camo hats shoots pool, while a lone geezer on the end of the bar watches a baseball game on one of the wall-mounted televisions.

Holt takes a seat at the opposite end of the bar. The bartender, a lanky fellow in a bleach-stained Grateful Dead t-shirt, sets down his wordsearch and plods over to him.

"Yuengling," Holt mutters, "and a shot of Jack."

Moments later the bartender sets the drinks in front of him and returns to his puzzle, all without a word. Holt studies them, the thin layer of frost on the bottle, the liquor's smooth amber shade. His armpits are damp. More things are coming loose in him, he can sense it, pieces of himself he'll never be able to reclaim, and he doesn't know how to finagle them back into place. And what's really troubling is he isn't even sure he wants to. Being capable of change isn't the same as *wanting* to change—that's another one of the AA moderator's favorite expressions—and increasingly Holt is having a hard time seeing the point of doing the right thing when the outcome doesn't seem any different.

He shuts his eyes tight and downs the shot, the liquor singeing his gullet, and then chases it with the beer. Swallowing sends a flare up the side of his face but he ignores it, wiping his mouth with the back of his hand. After nearly a year of sobriety he soon begins to feel his muscles going liquid, his mind loosening like a deflating balloon. That old reckless hunger yawning in his gut. What he wants is to tear something down, or stitch something back together, he can't tell which.

The beer is gone within minutes, and Holt orders another round, and then another. He drinks until the last call bell rings out, by which point he's the only customer left. When the bartender, who's already started turning chairs over on tabletops, drops off the check, Holt, remembering that his phone is out of commission, says, "And call me a cab, will you?"

He has the driver drop him off at the shop. Emmitt keeps the sliding metal doors sealed with a chain and a combination lock, though lucky for Holt he has a habit of whispering the numbers to himself as he dials through them every morning. Once inside, Holt latches the trailer to the truck hitch and, working by the fragile glow of the floodlight, loads up the auger and nailgun and chainsaw and as many two-by-fours as the trailer can handle.

Navigating the snaky backroads is treacherous, his vision blurry and unsteady, the truck drifting in and out of the lane, but he manages to make it to the doublewide a half hour later without landing the vehicle in a ravine. He pulls into the driveway and cuts over through the crabgrass to the line of posts standing like sentries around the base of the hill. It's close to midnight, a yellow half-moon cowering behind a thin veil of clouds. The air smells like honeysuckle and fresh dirt. Gusts of wind stir the pines at the base of the hill as Holt drives around the perimeter depositing armloads of two-by-fours in the wet grass. Once he's unloaded them all he climbs out of the cab and grabs the nailgun from the bed.

The doublewide is far enough up the hill, he assumes, that the woman won't hear the gun's airy popping. Nailing up the rails proves tricky without Emmitt there to counterbalance them, and the alcohol percolating in his veins doesn't make it any easier, but it seems vital that the job be finished as soon as possible, with or without Emmitt. In fact soon he's fallen into a rhythm, a calming reverie. A man needs a goal, he's always believed this, even if that goal is building something for someone else. An unoccupied mind will get you into trouble—just ask anyone in Blue Ridge State Correctional. Problem is, the older you get the more out of reach those goals begin to seem: you just keep chasing them and chasing them, and how long can you do that before finally accepting the fact that you never had a shot in the first place? Figuring out which things to hold onto and which ones to let go, that's pretty much all a life comes down to.

"What are you doing?"

At the sound of the voice, Holt lets out a yip and wheels around to see a woman in a ratty brown robe standing in the grass, the breeze whipping her stringy brown hair across her face.

When he doesn't respond, just gawps at her as he waits for his nerves to stop ringing, she repeats the question: "I asked you what you're doing."

He scratches his head with the business end of the nailgun, swaying on his feet. He can't think of an answer that doesn't sound like a lie.

"Finishing this fence," he says.

"It's midnight."

"Yes, ma'am, I know."

"So, why are you out here at midnight?"

"I just want to get it done," he replies. "I didn't mean to wake you up. I'll leave if you want me to."

"You didn't wake me. I don't sleep too good." The woman seems to consider him for a moment. "You're drunk," she comments, though there's no recrimination in her voice, no hostility. She could just as easily be commenting on the weather.

Holt, toeing a stiff tuft of weeds with his boot, nods. "Yes, ma'am. A little."

She swipes the hair out of her eyes, revealing a pale and expressionless face, like an unfinished sketch. It reminds him of an old sci-fi movie he and Charmaine watched about alien slugs that attached themselves to the backs of peoples' necks and took over their minds. The people moved about as blank-faced as robots, doing the aliens' bidding.

Slowly, she turns her head to look beyond him toward the tree line at the bottom of the hill, a maneuver that seems to require a great deal of effort. She scratches the back of her thin wrist. "You hungry?"

"Ma'am?"

"Let me make you something to eat."

She begins back up the hill toward the house. Something about her aloofness makes Holt feel on edge, like being in the wicked calm of a hurricane's eye, but he's not in a position to refuse her, so he drops the nailgun and brushes the sawdust off his shirt and follows her up the slope and up the rickety stairs into the doublewide.

The place looks as if it's been ransacked, the floors buried beneath a crust of dirty dishes, junk mail, and fast food cartons. He has to step over an overturned plant stand to make it into the living room. Piles of clothes clog the small hallway between there and bedroom. On the cluttered coffee table, a green ceramic ashtray blooms over with cigarette butts. The fetid smell of old grease and smoke hangs thickly. Amidst the mess Holt notices a scattering of kids' toys, action figures and plastic trucks and crumpled coloring books and, in the corner of the room, a rollercoaster table, the multicolored wires spiraling and loop-de-looping like the trajectories of flies. Kaylee has one, too, although as with most of her toys it only took her a few weeks to lose interest in it. Now Charmaine uses it to air dry her tops.

The woman, however, seems completely unfazed by the filth. "Here," she says, guiding him over to the counter. "Have a seat." She pulls back one of the stools and pushes off a stack of old coupon mailers. Then she drifts over to the cubby-sized kitchen on the other side and begins riffling through the fridge. Photos of a young boy, auburn-haired and sweetly dimpled, hang from alphabet magnets on the front. In one image, he stands at the tiled edge of a pool smiling up at the camera, a pair of orange floaties on his stubby arms. For some reason, Holt finds it hard to look away.

"Sorry for the mess," the woman says. "We don't get a lot of visitors."

"It's no problem."

"How do you like your eggs?"

"You really don't need to go to any trouble."

"Scrambled okay?"

"Sure, that's fine."

He watches her rummage through a cabinet for a bowl and whip the yolks with a whisk, her face maintaining its droopy-eyed gloss. From her thin, delicate features Holt can tell that she was once beautiful. Now her eyes, dark and deep-set, are edged by deep creases, like the grain of old wood. Veins the same bluish shade as mold mottle her forehead. Her dirty hair frames her face, the front of her robe open just enough to reveal the gaunt knobs of her collarbone.

"Ten years I been living here, and no one ever said anything about a fence," she says as she dumps the scrambled yolks into a pan. Holt gets the impression she isn't necessarily speaking to him. "Now the county wants to sue me for neglect."

"I'm sorry," he says dumbly.

"They act like a fence would make a difference. Like a kid couldn't just climb over it. Or under it."

"I guess they're just trying to cover their own asses."

She pushes the congealing mixture around the pan with a spatula. "Nothing surprises me anymore. You start to think the world is one way, and then you can't see it any other way, no matter how hard you try."

"It's not your fault what happened." Holt isn't sure why he's saying this, or even whom he's addressing, but he knows all the same that it needs to be said.

"County says it is. They're probably right. See, my boy, he's autistic, he don't understand when something's dangerous. He just *does* things. Once, I caught him wandering down the driveway in his underpants, told me he was walking to Wal-Mart. Can you believe that? He was dead serious, too. I think he woulda done it if I hadn't caught him, walked ten miles to goddamn Wal-Mart. When he gets an idea in his head, he's like a machine, see."

She dishes the eggs out onto a plastic plate and sets them in front of Holt and hands him a fork from the rack in the sink. When she isn't looking, he wipes the gunk off on his pants.

"I don't know where he was going that day," she continues, lighting up a cigarette, her eyes fixed on a point somewhere on the other side of the room. "All I know is I left him watching one of his videos and I went to the bathroom, and when I came out he was gone."

"How old was he?"

"He's four. You want any salt or pepper?"

"No thank you."

From the other side of the counter, the woman watches him with that flat, glazed look as he gobbles down the eggs in only a few forkfuls, and once more Holt recalls those alien slugs manipulating men and women around like puppets, steering them through their own lives, and he considers, distantly, whether or not the people were any worse off for it.

"How are they?" she asks, blowing a jet of smoke toward the ceiling.

"They're good."

"You really going to finish that fence tonight?"

"I don't know. That was the plan."

"You're tired."

And it's not until she says it that Holt realizes how true it is. The booze is burning out of his system, leaving him feeling drained and hollow. His eyes sting with drowsiness, and the knot on his face aches. All at once, finishing the fence on his own seems like an insurmountable obstacle, a trap he's wandered into.

"Why don't you lay down for a while?" she says. Floating over to the sofa, the woman sweeps the heaps of dirty clothes and old paperbacks onto the floor with one arm. She grabs a throw pillow out of the mess and places it against one of the armrests, giving it a friendly pat.

"I should get back," Holt replies, though not even he's buying it. "I'm not supposed to be here."

"Driving's the last thing you need to be doing. Sleep it off. Over here, come on."

With some hesitation, he wades his way through the junk on the floor to the couch, a weary weight already settling into his limbs. Easing himself down, he curls up on his side to keep his feet from dangling over the edge. The upholstery smells like sweat and unwashed hair, but he doesn't care. It's just good to be off his feet.

"There you go," the woman says, her voice softer now, tenderer, as she covers him with a quilt from the back of the sofa. "The fence will still be there when you wake up. Just rest." She brings a fingertip to the reddened lump on his jaw. "What happened here?"

"An accident," Holt answers, tucking the quilt beneath his chin. "A dumb one."

"Is there any other kind?"

She takes a seat on the adjacent armchair, ashes her cigarette onto the mound of butts in the ashtray. Even with his eyes closed Holt can feel her watching him, waiting for him to drift off. Any other time this would bother him, but tonight he's comforted to know that someone is close by. He tries not to think about what will happen when he wakes up, what he'll tell Emmitt about having stolen the truck. He tries not to think about the dead kid, the one in the pictures, or about the two boys in the back of the Tercel, their pale faces receding into the distance as the car disappeared down the highway. And Kaylee, he tries not to think about her either, whether he'll ever see her again. Instead, he thinks about the fence, how immaculate it will look like when it's finished. He can see it in his mind clear as a photograph, the long wooden rails encircling the property like a pair of arms.

Retreat

Tim called it a men's retreat, a way of reacquainting ourselves with our collective masculine spirit. He and Andy and Paul had already taken part in several. "I think you might really get something out of it, Josh," he told me in that earnest way he had, like an evangelist vying for your soul. "Given your state of affairs, I mean." And while the image that first came to mind was of a bunch of jowly, pot-bellied stockbrokers prancing around a bonfire in loincloths, I had to admit that there was something strangely appealing about the phrase, *our collective masculine spirit*. It was like being invited into some secret society.

A camping trip, one night, the five of us: Tim, Andy, Paul, myself, and Dwayne who, at twenty-eight, was the youngest member of our group, younger than me by five years. He was a master's candidate in the history department where I worked as an adjunct instructor while completing my dissertation. Andy and Paul, with whom I had gone to college, were junior partners at the architecture firm where Tim was a senior partner. Over the past year, they had come to regard him with the kind of childlike enthusiasm usually reserved for cool older brothers.

We all met up at Tim's house and took his truck out to Troutville. A client of his who owned a few hundred acres of land had agreed to let us use it for the retreat. From Route 11, we took a small single-lane gravel service road over a series of grassy hills populated by tank-sized cows, until we came to a wall of pine trees. A rusty red cattle gate blocked the entrance to a narrow hunting trail. Tim parked the truck off to the side of the road and then we grabbed our gear and, skirting the gate, headed off into the woods.

As the five of us tromped through the trees, huffing under the weight of our packs and swatting at clusters of gnats, I imagined how unsuited for the outdoors we must have appeared. Andy and Paul were stocky in a way that made them almost indistinguishable. Carrying Paul's grimy red ice chest between them, they moved with the ungainliness of men who have not yet gotten accustomed to the extra weight that middle age had bestowed upon them. Dwayne was short and wiry enough to have been mistaken for a teenager, were it not for the pink patch of scalp visible through his prematurely thin blond hair, as well as the cigarette dangling from his lip.

In fact, of the five of us, Tim was the only one who appeared even moderately fit for such an endeavor. With his well-tended beard and his crisp red flannel—L.L. Bean, I guessed—he looked like a taller, lankier Bob Vila.

We exited the woods into a massive stretch of knee-high yellow grass. It was late May, and the air was unseasonably crisp, strong wind drifts sweeping through the field with a low hiss, making waves in the grass. Out in the distance near the center of the field stood a large oak tree, its trunk bowed sharply. Standing there alone amidst all that empty space, it looked like a single whisker on an otherwise freshly shaven face. Tim guided us through the sparse trail he and Andy and Paul had made over their previous trips. "There it is," he said, gesturing to a patch of dark ash encircled by large rocks—remnants of the fire pit.

We got to work setting up our tents, about a dozen yards from the trunk of the tree, as Tim instructed. "We'll want the shade, but we don't want any branches coming down on us in the night," he said as he tamped down a section of grass for his tent. Spreading mine out, I watched out of the corner of my eye as Tim, twenty or so feet away from me, pitched his small blue pup tent with an expediency that I found both impressive and a little irritating. I could picture him working through trials in his back yard, setting the thing up and then taking it down, over and over again, trying hard to affect the appearance of a seasoned outdoorsman.

Dwayne and I exchanged self-conscious smirks as we fumbled with the collapsible poles of our tents.

"I haven't done this since Boy Scouts," I said.

"I never made it past Webelos," he sniggered.

There was a kind of kinship between me and him, based largely on the fact that we worked together and therefore spent more time with each other than we did with the other three. But there was also a shared skepticism about the whole endeavor. Frankly, it was only after I had pleaded with him that he agreed to come along. "At the very least, it will be good for a laugh," I'd said, though really I just didn't want to be the only tenderfoot among the group.

The state of affairs to which Tim had been referring when he invited me on the retreat was the breakup with my girlfriend Christine four months prior, or more precisely, the cataclysmic depression I'd been slogging through ever since. She and I had been together for just over two years at the time, though over those last six months or so I had been preoccupied by my dissertation—an exposition of the black American soldiers who had defected to the Philippines during the Spanish-American War—which was nowhere near complete, despite the fact that my four-year academic stipend had already run out and I'd had to pay for the fifth year out-of-pocket. When I wasn't teaching, I was either writing or poring over moldy yellow hardbacks, scribbling notes for what I had once imagined would be a revolutionary commentary on the racial politics of nineteenth-century combat.

Christine, however, had begun to take my work ethic personally. "I think you use that goddamn paper as an excuse," she'd told me once after I had backed out of movie plans to catch a lecture at the university.

"An excuse for what?" I tried not to bristle at her referring to it as a *paper*.

"To not have to deal with the world, with us."

"I have no idea what you're talking about."

"My point exactly."

And so it should have come as no surprise the evening that, out in the parking lot of my apartment complex, she informed me that it was over. "We just want different things right now," she said with a calculated calmness. I begged her to reconsider, and to her credit she did cry, though the tears were strictly ceremonial, the pretense of a difficult decision.

Over the next couple weeks, I managed to convince myself that all Christine needed was space, an opportunity to step back and recognize how vital I was to her happiness. And so I threw myself into my work in order to get my mind off of her. I spent long hours at the school library, haunting the carrels, badgering the surly student workers for more toner. We were just taking a breather, I told myself. That was all.

In that time she began seeing someone else, a sheriff's deputy named Clint whom she had met months prior after her car had been broken into downtown. He was tall and broad-shouldered with a face like something out of a catalog—not like me, doughy and edging on short, with my weak chin and receding hairline. (I did a little internet snooping and found that he had served in Iraq and, a few years after joining the sheriff's department, had once rescued a teenage girl from a burning apartment building; the city had presented him with a medal.)

"So that's it?" I said to her over the phone. "You're just over me? Just like that?"

"Well Christ, Josh, it's not like you gave me much incentive to stick around."

Since then I'd been unable to crawl out of my head. At night in the cruel dark quiet of my bedroom I would torment myself with images of Christine and Clint having sex: Clint bending her over the edge of a massive four-post oak bed that looked like something out of a Victorian period film; Christine weeping with delight as one monstrous orgasm after another wracked her shapely, glistening body. Why did I do this to myself? Perhaps I believed I deserved it, that my misery was a product of my own doing, and as such I was obligated to endure it. And maybe on some level I believed that my willingness to do so might somehow redeem me, make me worthy of Christine's affections once more.

Naturally, all of this made me an excellent candidate for Tim's men's group. Joined by a sense of injustice over our failed relationships, we had come to question our masculinity, what sorts of men we were and what made us so. Tim was at the tail end of a nasty divorce that had dragged on for a year and a half; his wife Kathryn, forty-one, had left him for a thirty-two-year-old tattoo artist. There was still the lingering custody issue of their fifteen-year-old son, who currently lived with her and referred to Tim by his first name. Andy's ex-wife had remarried to a bicycle shop owner who did improv comedy on weekends. Paul's wife left him to go harvest beets on a Zen farm in California. As for Dwayne, he had recently broken up with his girlfriend of three years, a pharmacy technician named Jill who, for his birthday the previous year, had had a star named after him through a pop-up ad she'd come across online.

Needless to say we were a little enamored with Tim, his air of rugged intellectualism. Women would have called him "mysterious," the beard and those dark eyes, the measured way he spoke, as though everything he said had been planned out in advance. Since his divorce he had become a fanatical advocate of the men's liberation movement. Prior to meeting him, I wasn't even aware that there was such a thing, and so I was fascinated the first time I heard his lengthy harangue about *reverse gender discrimination* and the guilt that this had ingrained into the minds of all American men, the result, he claimed, of the *vilification of masculinity*. "Think about the Bible," he'd say with a smug scholarly timbre. "The devil. He's a *man*. In every major religion, evil is masculine.

I mean, you've got she-devils in other cultures, sure, but even that term—'she-devil'—that implies a female version of what we already take to be a male concept. So you tell me, how does that not suggest bias?" His philosophy was engineered in such a way as to assuage our feelings of inadequacy for not having lived up to the standards of the women we loved. It didn't occur to us at the time that this confusion we felt about our relationship troubles actually had very little to do with the women themselves. We were flawed men, we knew this, but by Tim's reasoning we could convince ourselves that these flaws were someone else's fault.

Tim built a fire using the branches the rest of us had scavenged from the woods. Andy and Paul and I stood nearby hoping to be needed in some way, while Dwayne sat on one of the logs, smoking. "And there you go," Tim said after a few moments as the fire quickly began to grow. Coming to his feet, he put his hands on his hips. "Yeah, that maple burns real good, doesn't it?" We nodded dutifully.

After a dinner of burgers and beers, during which we jabbered hollowly about jobs and movies—the kind of banter used to prolong entry into a much weightier issue—the conversation began to die down, and Tim suggested we get started. Clearing his throat, he said, "We all know why we're here. We've been hurt in some way, each of us, but we've been conditioned to believe that we're not supposed to feel that way, that it's our responsibility to just accept the pain as part of our role in society. Men don't feel, isn't that what our culture tells us?"

Solemn nods all around.

He continued: "But we *do* feel. We have feelings. We shouldn't have to keep them to ourselves. Real men know how to talk to each other openly. They know how to accept blame and reject it when it's placed on them unfairly. And I think we would all agree that we've been treated unfairly."

I had been dreading the prospect of Tim guiding us through a checklist of flighty new age exercises, trust falls and heart chakras and whatnot, but to my relief he had nothing like that in mind. His plan more or less was for us to sit around the fire and deconstruct, in great detail, the actions of the women who had hurt us. *Purging*, he called this. We stowed our phones in our tents, in accordance with Tim's singular rule ("Make sure they're turned off, fellas," he'd instructed), and then we went clockwise around the fire, beginning with Andy, seated on one of the logs a few feet away from me, his considerable gut slumping over his thighs like a sleeping animal. He had a wide panlike face and the sad beginnings of a ginger-colored beard. "Even now, I keep asking myself, *What could I have done to prevent any of it?* And I know there's really nothing I could have done, but the feeling's still there, you know? Like, this nagging sensation that I did something wrong or missed something or whatever." He described the dissolution of his marriage—the months spent sleeping in separate beds, the divorce proceedings. "I always took the blame for everything, even when I knew it wasn't my fault. Not Susan, though, no way. She was *never* wrong. Eventually, I started to actually believe it, that it all really was my fault, but now I see that I was just being duped the whole time."

Paul, who was sporting a black combover and sprigs of hair protruding from beneath the collar of his t-shirt, rehashed the story of his divorce, craftily glossing over the part about the Applebee's waitress with whom he'd spent a couple weeks trading dirty text messages—"It was a stupid thing to do, I admit, but it's not like I fucked the girl"—and languishing over his then-wife Connie's refusal to go to marriage counseling—"I did everything I could to salvage it, the marriage, I made it clear to her that I wanted it to work, but she wouldn't even try." By the time he reached the point in the story where he'd relocated to the cramped loft downtown sans his plasma screen television and his Honda motorcycle (Connie had taken those in the divorce), he was sniveling like a child. We sipped our beers and listened and then offered up our syrupy platitudes, how it wasn't his fault, she just hadn't been receptive to his needs. The fact that these were the very same reassurances we so desperately wanted to hear from others lent them a disingenuous ring, but it still seemed to make Paul feel better, and that was all that mattered.

And in fact, we all seemed to feel better as the conversation progressed, at least more so than we had over the past few months— even Dwayne who, after some coaxing, recounted his last few days with Jill and even allowed himself to get a little choked up when he described the pain of having lost someone who had become such an integral part of his daily routine that he had had to relearn how to be alone.

"It hurts not having her around anymore," he said, swallowing back a sob, "but there's nothing I can do about it. I can't keep living in the past."

Of course the alcohol made the whole thing easier too, all the talking and sharing, all that *openness*, so that by the time my turn came around I found myself wonderfully alight with the spirit of the evening, drunk on brandy and beer and a rich sense of catharsis as I relayed to the other four men what had happened between Christine and me, a story we were all familiar with; we had all but memorized one another's tales of woe by this point. Nonetheless, as I spoke into the heat of the crackling fire, it felt fresh.

"I realize it's not really even about her," I said, a minor slur seeping into my voice. "It's about me, like, the way I see myself, this fear of, like, I don't know how to say it, of, like, just not being good enough. For anyone, not just Christine."

"You feel like you were replaced," Paul drawled, popping the cap of a fresh beer. It foamed over onto his hand, and he sucked his fingers.

"Yes! That's totally it! Because you'd think it would take longer for her to go and start screwing someone else. And it makes me wonder if maybe I'm the one with the problem here. I just don't understand how I'm sitting here obsessing, and she's totally over me like that." I snapped my fingers.

"It's just a rebound, dude," Andy reassured me.

Dwayne added "Or maybe she just wants to piss you off."

"Doesn't matter what the reason is," Tim interjected with a note of reproach. "Clearly, she's acting under this belief that men don't have the same feelings that women have, that we shouldn't feel things in the same way." We all looked at him, anxious to see how he would follow this up. In a sharp professorial tone, he said, "Seems we've all been conditioned to feel this way, in one way or another. We are fixers, the *doers*. So, when something goes wrong, it's on us to take the blame, isn't it? It's the role we've carved for ourselves."

I wasn't sure how he had arrived at this understanding, but I didn't want to sabotage the momentum of the discussion by contradicting him.

"I'm sorry, but that seems a little reductive," Dwayne commented. Andy and Paul glowered at him as though he'd spoken out of turn, and I couldn't help but feel a small pang of defensiveness on his behalf. He continued: "I'm not saying it's, like, wrong or anything. I just think that you can't place all the blame on women. I mean, no offense to anyone here or anything, but I don't know—it takes two people to make a relationship. It doesn't seem healthy to assume that it's all on their shoulders."

Quickly, I looked back at Tim to see whether or not he would let this throw him off balance. Instead, he simply nodded and scratched his temple, regarding Dwayne like a kid who had just said something adorable.

"Well, I hear what you're saying, and I agree it would be reductive to place all the blame on women. But see, it's not just an issue of blame.

I'm not claiming that they, women I mean, are somehow to blame for all this—whatever." He emphasized this last part with a flutter of his fingers. "All I'm saying is that they never really see us for who we are, because we've been taught to hide it."

Out of the corner of my eye, I noticed Paul and Andy exchange a victorious smirk.

Dwayne scratched his head and reached for his cigarettes on the ground. "Yeah, I guess that makes sense," he said, though I could tell he wasn't buying it.

It went on like this for some time, the talking and the drinking, our voices echoing across the field, until eventually the conversation deteriorated into teary proclamations of brotherly affection, the five of us raising our bottles in a toast around the fire.

"You guys are my family," Paul sputtered, "like, you don't even know. I love you guys so much." Andy tried to get us all going on a chorus of "Let It Be," but no one could remember all the words.

Tim must have felt that his having moderated the discussion precluded him from the purging process, because in all of the drunken revelry, nobody thought to ask him to tell his story. Instead, he sat there against his log, his head bobbing from the booze, grinning like a doting parent. After a while, when nobody else had brought it up, I decided it best to let it go, mostly because I didn't want to spoil the moment, but also because something told me he had orchestrated things to play out this way.

It was after midnight by the time we staggered off to our tents, leaving the fire to smolder into the night. The purging had left me too wired, too full of questions to sleep. I checked my phone. A couple texts from friends, but nothing from Christine. Not that I was surprised. It had been over two months since I'd heard from her, but still I couldn't help wondering where she was right then, what she was doing. Probably she was fucking Clint. In my head, she was always fucking Clint. Every minute of every day. Was he better at it than me? I could see her making mental notes to herself as he ravaged her, of all the ways in which his skills exceeded mine. I missed our little rituals, the way that she and I used to pad out to the kitchen after sex, naked and slippery, and eat ice cream out of the container by the coppery glow of the stove light. Did she do this with him, too? Did they have their own rituals yet?

After a while I slipped on my shorts and a sweatshirt and battled my way out of the tent to go pee. The night was cool and rich with the trill of crickets. Stumbling out past the oak tree, I urinated into the tall grass. As I was finishing up, I heard a cough from somewhere close behind me. I wheeled around to see Tim slumped against the base of the tree, his feet splayed and his hands resting on his belly. He appeared to be holding something, a photo of some sort judging from the shape of the object, but it was too dark to make out the image. I hadn't bothered to grab a flashlight when leaving the tent, and had it not been for his white undershirt, I might not have even spotted him there in the shadows.

"Hey," he said with a nervous laugh, raising a hand in greeting. "Did I scare you? Sorry."

"It's okay."

"It was a good discussion tonight, huh?" he said. The words were flat and jumbled together in a way that told me he was still smashed.

"Yeah. Really productive. Made me think a lot."

"Good."

He stood, tottering slightly, and walked to me, his body hunched, his arms limp at his sides. He seemed like a completely different person than the staid, self-possessed character who had guided us through the purging.

"You okay?" I said.

He nodded and ran the backs of his fingers along his furry jaw. "Just doing a little—what's the word? Self-reflection. I guess."

"Gotcha."

When he saw me looking at the photo, he handed it to me. "That's my wife. Jessica. I mean my ex-wife. Probably can't see it too good in the dark."

Actually, the silvery sliver of moon lent just enough light for me to make out the image: Tim and a black-haired woman with a prim aquiline nose sitting together in a bar booth, both of them smiling laughingly at the camera. He was wearing a blazer, she a spaghetti strap dress. The photo was rumpled and bent enough to suggest that he'd been carrying it around for some time.

"She's pretty," I said for lack of anything else to say.

Nodding, he sighed. "Seventeen years I was married, man. It's crazy, huh? Nights are really the hard part. That's when it really hits you, the loneliness."

"I know what you mean."

"The guys at the firm, they're all like, 'You should go find somebody, get back out there, date around.' All that crap. But it's deeper than that, you know? It's not about just going out and finding some *woman*." He didn't say the word so much as spit it out like an insect that had flown into his mouth. "I think one of the worst feelings in the world is knowing that you're just something that's happened to somebody. And I'm so tired of that."

Something that's happened to somebody. That was a good way to put it. How much sleep had I lost panicking over the idea that Christine's eagerness to move forward with her life spoke much less about her character than it did mine? How much of our lives are spent desperately hoping for someone to return our affections?

"I know it's kind of weird, all this emotional stuff," he said, sweeping an unsteady hand through the air. "It's hard to be open with each other. Guys, I mean." There was a distant quality to his voice, as though he didn't entirely believe what he was saying. Maybe it was the booze, but I couldn't be certain. "But I really appreciate you coming out here. And bringing Dwayne. Because, you know, we're all hurting in some way, and we'd like to think that keeping it to ourselves is, like, the manly thing to do, you know?"

"Sure. Yeah."

We were quiet for some time. The wind hummed and the crickets creaked all around us. For some reason, my thoughts drifted back to my dissertation, those disenfranchised soldiers shipped off to the Philippines to fight for a country that had never offered them any sense of belonging. *JOIN US!* proclaimed the pamphlets that the insurrectos would post conspicuously in the villages. *YOUR MASTERS HAVE THROWN YOU INTO AN INIQUITOUS BATTLE! THE FILIPINOS ARE YOUR FRIENDS!* The fact of the matter is that just because you love something, that doesn't mean it has to love you back.

A breeze rolled through, snapping at my sleeves and tousling my hair. Tim and I were standing only a few feet apart at this point, close enough for me to smell the smoke in his clothing. He put his hand on my shoulder as if to console me and began kneading the tender region between the joint and my neck. I chuckled, but not because I thought it was funny.

"I care about you, Josh. Seriously. I care about all you guys. I need you."

I nodded.

I would like to say that what came next was a complete surprise, but I suppose that in some region of my mind I must have recognized the soft lilt of his voice for what it was, the pressure of his body so close to mine, and I understood that whatever was about to happen, I wasn't going to stop it.

Without a word, he ran his hand up to my face and cupped my cheek and, taking an abrupt step forward, kissed me. It was a hard, sloppy maneuver, hurried, as if there were some chance of us getting caught. But who was there to catch us? Andy and Paul and Dwight were all snoring in their tents a few yards away, and beyond that there was just the lonely expanse of the field. This is what I was thinking as he cupped the back of my head and pulled me to him, how alone we were out here in the cool darkness, no one around to hear him groan as he piled his tongue into my mouth with an adolescent's clumsy ardor, nobody to see the way he began working his jaw against mine as though he intended to devour me, or how I didn't stop him, didn't push him away, no, but instead sank greedily into the kiss, wrapping my arms around his shoulders and pulling myself to him.

Where did it come from, this sudden hunger for Tim's mouth, for his body? It seemed to blossom out of some larger abstract need for validation, one that had less to do with Christine than it did with the way I perceived myself as a component of the world, and in an instant all of the self-pity and confusion and despair and doubt, those things that had accumulated in me like engine grime, they were forgotten, and when Tim, his gamey-smelling body pressed tightly against mine, ran his palm down my stomach and then between my legs, I didn't stop him. Instead, I gave into it, the motion of his hand against my erection, his sour breath on my neck as I titled my head back in a moan. I angled my pelvis into his hand, I let it happen, and in a searing flash my mind went blank.

Then it was over. Less than a minute, maybe. Tim's hand lingered between my legs, but his groping had stopped. He was panting into my ear, heavy and dismayed. I stepped back and I looked him over, the long severe lines of his face. I felt cold and empty and dry, the same way I had felt after Christine had left. Tim was sort of swaying, hands now at his sides, palms out. He appeared frozen, like he was in shock. He felt it, too, I could tell, that whatever we'd been reaching for was only an illusion, a bubble burst by the slightest touch, tenuous enough to make you wonder if it had ever really been there at all.

Finally, I took a breath and smoothed back my hair, and then without a word I shuffled past him toward my tent, leaving him there beneath the tree, a hunched figure in the dark. After a few steps I realized that I was still holding the photo, but something told me to just keep moving, so I just crammed it in my pocket.

The sun was cresting above the tree line the next morning when I crawled out of my tent, and there was a smoky chill in the air. Birds twittered in the distance. My head throbbed dully and my mouth felt sticky and foul. The events of the night before seemed faded and far-off, like remnants of a dream. I didn't know what to make of what had happened. Too much alcohol, I wanted to tell myself, but that seemed too easy, a cheat.

Dwayne was already up, seated on one of the stumps by the fire in a pair of shorts and a hooded sweatshirt, his knees drawn up to his chest. A saucepan of water sat atop a few of the remaining embers.

"Morning," I said, trying to sound as casual as possible.

"Hey. Thought I'd go ahead and get coffee started."

"How long have you been up?"

"About forty-five minutes, maybe an hour." He peered into the pan.

"Couldn't sleep, or what?"

He offered a tight smile, as if I had just told an off-color joke. Licking his lips, he reached into his pocket for his cigarettes. "Jill texted me last night," he said as he lit up.

"Really?"

"Yeah. We talked for like two hours."

I waited a couple beats before saying, "And?"

He sighed. "She wants to get together and talk. You know, about *us*. Says she misses me." He said this as though the words had a bad taste.

"Well, that's a good sign, right?"

"See, that's the thing. It's like, yeah I miss her, too, but what good would it do, getting back together? Would we really be better off?"

I mulled this over for a moment. "This doesn't sound at all like the stuff you've said in the past." I was doing my best not to sound disappointed. Where was all the dreary preteen sentiment, the desperation, the heartache? I couldn't help feeling betrayed, as though he had broken some pact we had made to be miserable together.

Shrugging, he said, "It was something about last night, you know, all the talking around the fire. I started wondering, if me and Jill did get back together, would either one of us really be better off? Or are we just terrified of being alone?"

He had a point, I guess. I'd wondered this too, whether Christine was *someone*, an anchor, and I wanted to believe that this was reason enough to hold onto her. Because isn't this what it always comes down to? Familiarity versus the unknown? Aren't most of us just looking for a distraction from ourselves?

"Look, do me a favor," Dwayne said. He glanced over at the other three tents as if to make sure the others were still sleeping and then leaned in close to me. "Don't get too sucked into this stuff."

"What stuff?"

"All this men's liberation crap. I know these guys are your friends, but you don't need this. We'd like to think we're victims here, but that's not really true, and you know it. You're not going to get anywhere by just being pissed off at women."

"I'm not pissed off."

"We're all pissed off, Josh. And that's fine. But this isn't therapy. It's a bunch of dudes sitting around the woods blaming women for all their problems. Tim? He's an okay guy, but he's just as screwed up as we are. Only difference is, he doesn't see it. I'm only saying this because you're my friend. You don't need this."

I looked out across the field toward the dark curtain of trees. Everyone else seemed to know what I needed. Why didn't I?

"I think I'm going to go for a walk," I mumbled. Suddenly I didn't want to be there when the others woke up. Especially Tim.

Dwayne nodded as if in sympathy and turned his attention back to the pan.

Walking out into the field, I let the tall dewy grass swish against my bare legs. I was close to the tree line that marked the edge of the field when I remembered Tim's photo in my pocket. I took it out and studied it. There he was, smiling brightly at the camera, a man with things to look forward to. My guess was that the picture hadn't been taken more than just a few years before, but still something about that smile and the way his hand was resting on his wife's bare shoulder made him appear much younger, almost unrecognizable.

I was trying not to think about what would happen later on, after we had cleaned up the site and headed back into town. After we had returned to our glum little lives. I tried not to think about Tim, whether he and I would even speak again once all of this was over. It's frustrating business, the future, all that waiting around to just get it over with.

And I guess it was this frustration that compelled me to crumple up the photo and chuck it as hard as I could into the trees, like a piece of trash. Somehow I knew that Tim wouldn't come asking for it.

A couple minutes later I heard the muted din of voices echoing back to me. Looking back toward the campsite, I saw that the others were up. They sat around the fire pit, the four of them, sipping coffee and chatting.

Tim glanced over in my direction for a few moments. I couldn't tell if he was looking directly at me or not, but I suspected that he was, and I knew that the only progress we had made was realizing the scope of our own desperation. His words from the previous night echoed in my head, *becoming something that happened to somebody.* At some point, I suppose we all become someone else's failure. Someone told a joke and they all laughed. From where I stood out in the field with my back to the woods, they were indistinct figures, blips of color against the horizon, small enough to be mistaken for children.

The Future is Not for Sale

Ken McKinnon wandered along the craggy two-mile stretch of road that connected the Matthews house to the highway. At his side he carried a half-finished six-pack to keep up the buzz he'd been maintaining for the past four days. That was when he and Nina had driven down from D.C. at the advice of his lawyer, Gwen. She was a severe woman with a pageboy haircut and a seemingly endless supply of earth-toned pantsuits. "I'm going to file a few pretrial motions to buy us some time," she'd explained over the phone. "It wouldn't surprise me if the judge dismisses the case altogether, the county's process service was so screwy. In the meantime, try to relax. You've earned it." Ordinarily, the house was the ideal place to relax, a white A-frame nestled in a woodsy lot five miles outside the fishing hamlet of Matthews, Virginia, with a wraparound deck that offered a panoramic view of the Chesapeake inlet. However, after nearly a week it was becoming clear that whatever Ken had hoped for out here, clarity or comfort, he wasn't going to get it.

On either side of the road were gassy-smelling marshlands where egrets and herons stalked for fish amidst the yellow reeds. Fiddler crabs crowded the scorching asphalt, scuttling away upon his approach. It wasn't until Ken heard the horn blaring behind him that he realized he'd staggered into the middle of the road. He barely had time to leap out of the way before a red pickup with rusted fenders and the words STREAMLINE GUTTERS FREE ESTIMATES printed on the side shot past. It missed him by inches, the heady whoosh of air making him stagger on the shoulder. An arm emerged from the window to give him the finger. Startled, Ken hurled the bundle of beers at the vehicle. He'd played baseball in college and apparently his pitcher's instincts hadn't left him completely, because the beers struck the back windshield almost dead center, leaving a spider web crack the size of a basketball.

The truck skidded to a stop, and a beefy fellow in a blue work shirt and tattered Nationals ball cap burst out of the cab. He was easily twice Ken's size, blocky as a vending machine, his balled-up fists like a pair of wrecking balls. He marched over to him. "The fuck is your problem?"

Ken had the same feeling he'd had the day the sheriff's deputies had shown up at the house, like he'd been shot with a stun gun, muscles zapped rigid. He glanced back and forth between the man and the truck parked crookedly in the road.

"It was an accident," he managed.

"Oh right, those cans just threw themselves? Shit, wasn't a damn accident!"

"I didn't think it would hit the glass."

Now the man was standing directly in front of him, and Ken had to crane his neck up to meet his eyes. He was young, early thirties maybe, though his face had the same timeworn character of all the men in the region. Long, sharp lines like eroded stone. It reminded him of how his old man had looked, particularly in his later years, his cheeks flattened and scored with creases from a lifelong campaign against smiling.

"It's my boss's truck," the man said. "He's going to take that shit out of my check."

"Here, I can give you my contact info, okay?" Still teetering from the combination of beer and the shock of having made such a fluky throw, Ken removed his wallet and handed the man a business card. His office number was printed at the bottom, though it wouldn't do him much good: in an effort to avoid a PR disaster, Ken's company, Magellan Foods, Inc., where he'd headed up the East Coast marketing division, had forced him into early retirement shortly after the allegations had arisen that he had embezzled seventy-thousand dollars from the Prince William County school board, for which he'd served as treasurer for nearly ten years. Ken jotted his cell number on the back of the card and handed it over. He added, "I am sorry, I don't know what I was thinking. I'll take care of it, okay?"

The man examined the card suspiciously, appearing to lower his guard a little. "Look, I don't know where you're from, dude," leveling a fat finger at him, "but you'd better watch yourself. You're liable to get your ass kicked pulling this shit, y'hear?"

Ken glanced around at the mucky grasslands to either side of him as if searching for a reply. He was aware of how the locals saw out-of-towners, like a mass of well-to-do zoo-goers ogling the innocent animals. In his defense, throwing the cans had been a reflex, nothing more. He hadn't intended to hit the windshield, and paying for it wouldn't be a problem. Nonetheless, something in the warning troubled him. It made him think of all the harassment he and Nina had endured since the indictment, like how someone had spray-painted the word "THIEVES" onto their driveway in jagged red letters, or the bistro maître d' who had refused to seat them last week, threatening to call the cops if they didn't leave. "We don't deserve to be treated like this," Nina had protested. "We didn't do anything."

But the chemical blonde in the too-tight sweater simply crossed her skinny arms and said, "As far as I'm concerned, ma'am, you pretty much did."

Before it occurred to him what he was doing, Ken snatched the ball cap off the man's head and then bolted clumsily into the marsh, losing a shoe in a pocket of mud. Behind him, he could hear the fellow's furious shouts, but he didn't look back. He just kept crashing through the tall yellow grass, scaring up birds like fireworks.

That evening as the sun was setting, Ken sat in a deck chair turning the hat over in his hands. It was weathered stiff with sweat and salt, the bent bill faded. Its smell was a combination of dirt and oil, pungent but not unpleasant, and there was a fishhook clipped to the underside of the bill. What had compelled him to take it? Nerves, most likely. He hadn't been in a fight since he was a boy, and who knew what a man that size was capable of? Ken was sixty-three, with a modest gut even in spite of the three miles a day he walked, and his mahogany hair had taken on the grayish tint of cigarette ash. His days of picking fights were long over. Still, he was embarrassed by the whole thing, grabbing the hat off the guy's head and then scampering away like that, a coward. It was the sort of impetuous move his old man might have scolded him for as a kid.

The elder McKinnon used to bring Ken and his two older brothers Cameron and Collin out to the Mathews house when they were boys. The four of them would spend languorous summer weekends catching drum off the pier, a welcomed break from the raucous sprawl of Alexandria, Virginia, where Ken's father was a corporate tax attorney. In his day-to-day life the old man was gruff, short-tempered. He was someone who took comfort in predictability—this, Ken suspected, was how he'd wound up in his profession, because there was a kind of assurance in the endless numbers and formulae, the tables and graphs. They were an absolute. But out here, in the unassuming berg of fishermen and crabbers and oyster farmers and mechanics and carpenters and grocery store clerks, the old man's crustiness always seemed to abate, for a little while anyway.

In fact, Ken too had always found himself less inhibited in Mathews. Perhaps it was all the open space, not like back home where you worked hard to avoid physical contact in public, and where even the trees felt artificial somehow, municipal ornaments. Here you had more freedom than you knew what do to with. He recalled the time Collin snagged a mammoth striped bass, fifteen pounds easy with green and black scales that shone like chrome in the afternoon sun, only to have it wriggle out of his hands as he was fumbling with the hook. Ken, eight at the time and always eager to show off for his brothers, dashed into the inlet to retrieve the fish but ended up slicing his foot on a rock. The cut wasn't much worse than the errant slice of a dull paring knife, but at the time it felt like his foot had been cleaved in two, painful enough that his father had to wade in to get him and then carry him back up to the house, where he doused the wound with hydrogen peroxide.

"What'd you think was going to happen, running into the water like that?" the man said. They were in the upstairs bathroom, Ken perched on the sink basin with his bloodied foot on the toilet lid. "You don't know what's in there."

"I was trying to catch the fish," Ken spluttered. His face was raw with tears and snot, not so much from the pain but from spoiling the tranquil afternoon.

His father doused the cut again, and Ken swallowed back a sob as the wound sizzled with foam. The man said, "Yeah? Well, look how that worked out."

Behind him, the sliding glass door opened, snapping Ken back into the present, and Nina stepped out onto the porch. "Where'd you get that?" she said, motioning to the hat.

"Found it."

"Where?"

"On the road." It wasn't a total lie, but Ken still couldn't bring himself to meet her eyes.

"Gwen called while you were out."

"What did she say?"

"Wants you to call."

"Okay."

When he didn't say anything else, Nina added, "You want me to bring you the phone, or what?"

"I'll call her later."

"It's getting late, Ken. You don't want to wait too long."

"Christ, Nina, I said I'd call her, alright? She's *my* lawyer."

Nina lifted her palms in her just-trying-to-help gesture and then lumbered back inside the house. Out on the horizon, the fishing boats were trawling back to shore for the day. A dog barked somewhere in the pines encircling the property, the sound bouncing across the water.

Back in March a county bookkeeper had noticed the seventy-thousand-dollar discrepancy in the school board coffers. As investigators soon discovered, someone had been cashing checks illegally for over a year. As treasurer, Ken was one of the first people the authorities looked at. Just procedure, they'd assured him. No problem, he was happy to comply. Other than a couple parking tickets, his record was sparkling. But stories of this sort had a way of stoking the fury of a community that, only a thirty-minute drive from Capitol Hill, was increasingly hostile to misuses of power, and within hours of Ken's indictment news vans descended upon his and Nina's quiet D.C. suburb, antennae towers hoisted like upraised fists. At his arraignment, the two of them were greeted outside the courthouse by a clamorous mob of student protestors. Ken's was just the latest in a long string of white collar cases in the region, each one more high-profile than the last, and the protestors carried signs with vaguely oppositional sayings like *THE FUTURE IS NOT FOR SALE!!!* Ken had no idea what this meant, but he was under strict orders from Gwen not to engage with the crowd, just keep his eyes down and keep moving.

And yet throughout the ordeal, he had maintained his innocence. He'd never stolen a thing in his life, he assured the county investigators during his deposition, why would he start now? Plus, as the Board president pointed out in a huffy letter to the judge—sent in spite of Ken's protestations—in his nine years of service, Ken had been reelected three times by comfortable margins. *Clearly, people in this community trust*

Mr. McKinnon, the letter proclaimed. *What reason could he have for wanting to violate that trust?*

Ken drove through the gate of the eight-foot chain link fence surrounding Streamline Gutters and pulled into the graveled parking area. The building was a charmless steel shell with a single unmarked door. Inside, he found an provisional office area comprising a collection of cluttered sheet metal desks and, off to the side, a foldable table with an ancient coffee maker on top. In the far back were pallets of metal slats waiting to be shaped, as well as a couple of coffin-shaped machines intended, presumably, to do exactly that.

At the moment, however, none of them were running. The whole place was silent, the makeshift office area empty.

"Hello?" Ken called out.

A fat man with a scraggly mustache appeared from the back. "Hey," he said to Ken, squashing out a cigarette on the cement floor. Ken must have caught him during a smoke break. "What can I do for you?"

"I'm looking for a guy who works here. I think he does, anyway. Big guy, drives a red truck?"

"That's Wyatt." The man nodded to one of the desks piled high with old invoices and receipts and fast food wrappers. There was a handwritten placard taped to the front: *Wyatt Sutton.* "Got him out doing an estimate right now. Anything I can help you with?"

"I wanted to give this to him." Ken held up the cap, which he'd been clutching nervously with both hands.

"You can leave it on his desk. Dunno when he'll be back."

"I would really prefer to give it to him myself, if it's all the same."

A sudden stiffness came over the man's face, his pouchy eyes narrowing. "You're the one who vandalized my truck, aren't you?"

"I wasn't aiming for your truck, I swear."

"I oughta call the police on your ass right now. You know that whole windshield's gonna have to be replaced?"

"Please. I told—Wyatt, is that his name? I told him I'd pay for it. I gave him my card. I want to make things right, okay? I just came by to bring him his hat."

The man scratched the back of his bulbous head, which was ringed with gray curls. His whiskery jowls twitched in uncertainty. He waddled around to the front of the desks and considered Ken for a long moment. "Where you from, dude?"

"Alexandria."

"Alexandria." He repeated the word the way an angry parent might parrot a lying child. "Long way. What are you doing down here?"

Ken cleared his throat. "My family's had property here for years."

"That don't mean you belong." There it was again, the insinuation that he was somehow too much of an outsider. Exactly how large was the gulf between his life here and the one back home?

"Excuse me," he rebutted, "but I've been coming here since before you were even born."

"Then you oughta know better, huh?"

Ken didn't reply. He shifted his focus to the clutter on Wyatt Sutton's desk. There was an assortment of pictures taped to the wall behind the battered office chair: Sutton in a hooded camo jacket, kneeling in the grass beside a deer he'd just killed. A pretty redhead Ken guessed to be the man's wife. School portraits of two freckle-faced girls, eight years old or so. There was an article that Ken had read somewhere that claimed the condition of a person's workspace was as telling as any personality inventory, and while he couldn't recall exactly what a junky desk was supposed to say about a person, he guessed there must have been something to it because as he surveyed Sutton's workspace Ken had the unaccountable sense that he'd known this fellow for ages.

The man fished a fresh cigarette out of his front shirt pocket. It hadn't been ten seconds since he finished the previous one. With the cockiness of a movie gangster, he released a billow of smoke, coughing wetly into his fist. "You can leave the hat on Wyatt's desk if you want," he said as he ambled back toward the shadowy rear of the shop. "I'll see that he gets it."

Ken spent the rest of the afternoon on into the evening cruising along the coastal backroads, past long watery tracts of cypress trees and marinas where gulls congregated hungrily on the gangways. He stopped for a drink at a ramshackle bar that doubled as a bait shop during the day. By the time he made it home, he could hear Nina's wheezy snores coming from the bedroom. Ever since the indictment, she'd maintained a regimen of Klonopin and red wine, zonking out at 7:00 PM and waking up at noon. In the kitchen, he found a note on the counter: *Gwen called—AGAIN.* The last word was underlined three times. Ken grabbed a beer from the fridge to steel his nerves and then, resigning himself to the fact that he'd put his attorney off as long as he could, picked up the cordless phone. Because cell phone coverage was spotty this far out in the boonies, he'd insisted that Gwen use the landline.

"Jesus, Ken," she said, "I was about to call the cops down there to go looking for you."

"Keeping myself busy, is all."

"Doing what, dodging my calls?"

"No. Just stuff around the house."

"Well, you should probably start packing it in. The case is going to trial."

He sank down hard into a slatback chair next to the fridge. "But you said you'd be able to get it dismissed."

"No, what I said was there's a good chance it would be," she retorted in her coolly-calm lawyer's tone. "But that's just the way these things go, c'est la vie and whatnot, you know? Anyway, we've got a little bit less than a month to prepare, so I'm going to need to sit down with you to go over these statements you gave to the police."

"A *month*, that's all?"

"We'll be okay if we can get to it ASAP. I still think we have a good shot here, but we need to get to work, like, yesterday, you hear me?"

After he'd gotten off the phone with Gwen, Ken padded to the bedroom and peeked in at Nina, dozing into her pillow. She was short and thickly built, especially in the chest and hips, and she had a pleasantly plump face that, even in her early sixties, gave her a demeanor of youthful gentility. Ken's father had always adored her, calling her "Sunshine" and doting on her as if she were his own. For this reason, it had become hard lately for Ken to look at her without his thoughts drifting disconsolately to the old man's last few years, which he'd spent in a nursing home, his mind dissolving from dementia. As the only son living nearby—Cameron was in South Carolina, and Collin was in Florida—Ken did his best to make it out there at least a couple times a week. Because the nurses insisted that conversation was good for his memory, particularly as the periods of clarity grew shorter and more infrequent, Ken would come prepared with a topic of small talk, something that he hoped might spark some dormant mental circuit.

One time he brought up the striped bass incident. "What bass?" the elder McKinnon replied after Ken had rehashed the scenario. The man was slumped in his ratty La-Z-Boy in a yellowed undershirt and jeans. His sunken eyes were the leaden hue of a thunderhead.

"Collin caught it," Ken said.

"Collin?"

"He's one of your boys, Dad. He was trying to take it off the hook, but he dropped it and I ran out into the lake to get it back, cut my foot pretty bad. You had to haul me back up to the cabin. We made a big joke about it, you remember?" In fact, it had become something of a credo within the family. *Don't go chasing any fish!* the old man would warn, teasing. Translation: *Don't do anything crazy.*

Ken's father studied him in narrow-eyed concentration as if he suspected that he was being tested. And for an instant Ken thought perhaps he saw something flit over his face, a glimmer of recognition, some measure of hope. But no, that must have been wishful thinking because a second later the man shifted his attention away, his face falling the way it did whenever he couldn't recall something he knew he should.

"I don't remember any damn fish," he grumbled.

Now Ken crept into the room and slid into bed next to his wife. She came awake with a groan, her eyelids creaking open a sliver.

"Did you call Gwen?" she whispered.

"Yes."

"Is everything okay?"

"Everything is fine."

She gave a groggy groan of confirmation and nuzzled her forehead against his shoulder.

"I took it," Ken said.

"I know, honey. You found the hat on the road."

From her voice it was clear that she was only fractionally conscious, and so he didn't bother correcting her that it wasn't the hat he was talking about, it was the seventy-thousand. He didn't explain to her how it had started with a single 300-dollar check from an elementary school PTA that he'd fraudulently cashed, a decision he had yet to comprehend, nor did he tell her about the ad hoc system of alternate accounts he'd cobbled together to disguise the continued theft, which, even despite his best efforts, he couldn't bring himself to stop.

Ken didn't say a word to his wife. Instead, he stroked her hair, soft and wavy and fragrant with her mango conditioner, until she fell back asleep.

It was almost 11:30 according to the dashboard clock when Ken pulled up the weedy drive of Wyatt Sutton's house. The place was a small white modular with a set of wooden steps built onto the front. A pair of stately walnut trees towered over it like sentries. Leaving the keys in the ignition, he crept out of the car toward the steps, trying to avoid the tufts of dead cheatgrass, which crunched underfoot. He mounted the steps and reached out to drop the cap at the front door. That was when the motion light came on. Ken froze, his elongated shadow cast out over the barren yard. His brain was shrieking at him to flee, but his muscles weren't receiving the message. The door swung open with a clatter, and there was Sutton himself, dressed in old basketball shorts and a t-shirt, his massive frame occupying the entirety of the doorway.

"What the fuck?" he growled when he spotted Ken frozen on the steps.

For a few seconds, all Ken could do was stare up at the man. Just drop off the hat and make a speedy getaway, that had been his plan. Couldn't have been simpler. He should have realized that simplicity was an illusion, too many variables lurking around, most of which go unconsidered until even the most rudimentary plans are thwarted. Mosquitoes needled his arms, but he couldn't summon the nerve to swat them away.

Sutton descended a single step toward him. "This is my home, man. What the hell are you doing here?"

With trembling hands, Ken finally held the cap out to him. "I wanted to bring this to you."

At first Sutton scowled at it, dismayed, then he snatched it out of Ken's hand. The same way you might snag a subpoena from a process server.

"How'd you even know where I live?"

"Google." The search had yielded legions of Suttons in the area, though thankfully only one W. Sutton.

"Dude, what is the matter with you, for real? Like, are you crazy or something?" It was clear this wasn't just a jab, the man was genuinely curious.

"I don't know." As if to drive the point home, the strength in Ken's legs disappeared all at once, and he collapsed with a thump onto his rear on the bottom step. He squeezed his eyes shut, willing himself not to cry, not in front of this man, but it was no use, the tears were already coming, hot and thick and as sharp as acid.

He buried his face in his hands. "I'm so sorry."

Sutton hunkered down with some reluctance on the step behind Ken, grunting with the effort it took to fold up his body. "Look, it's alright, I guess. I appreciate you bringing it back. No big deal, okay?"

Probably he was just trying to pacify this potentially unstable stranger, but Ken still couldn't stop his mind from going back to that afternoon in his father's nursing home room, the frantic need for the old man to remember his—Ken's—one stab at recklessness. To see him as someone who could act against self-interest. Maybe that was why he'd taken the money, not because he and Nina needed it, but because he wanted to see what would happen when he followed through on an impulse. And sure, his father would have harangued him for it like he had when he'd gone chasing after Collin's bass, and he would have been right to do so. But just look where his own sensibleness had landed him—in a dreary retirement home reeking of carpet cleaner and piss, his mind eroding as steadily as a floodplain. Had that sensibility made him any better off? Ken had asked himself this question more times than he could remember over the past few months, yet he still hadn't come up with a satisfactory answer.

Behind the two men, the screen door squeaked open, and the redhead from the picture on the wall behind Sutton's desk poked her head out. In the coppery glow of the porchlight, her ginger hair appeared to emit its own light. With her high, rounded cheekbones and vaguely protrusive ears, Mrs. Sutton made him think of Nina, the way she'd slipped her hand into his like a frightened child as they had shouldered their way through the crowd outside the courthouse. "You alright?" Mrs. Sutton said to her husband, giving Ken a suspicious glance.

"I think so."

"Need me to call somebody?" Her voice was just above a whisper, as if there was some chance of Ken, sitting right next to Sutton, not hearing her.

Sutton didn't answer right away. He gave Ken an appraising look, the same look Ken had seen on his father's face that day, hopeful and uncertain at the same time, a struggle against better judgment. The mosquitoes continued their assault on his arms and neck, but he hardly noticed them. He could feel Sutton and his wife watching him, deciding things, and all he could do was stare out into the dark expanse of trees where bullfrogs croaked in a low chorus, as he waited to find out what kind of man he was.

In the Jungle

A man always has two reasons for doing anything:
a good reason and the real reason.
   –J.P. Morgan

After fourteen years as the CFO of Magellan Foods, Inc., Collier was convinced that failure came in only two varieties: the middling stumbling blocks of human error, which could give you a headache but were at least manageable (botched spreadsheets, incompetent staff), and the colossal fuckups you read about on the cover of *Time*: Bear Stearns and AIG, Bernie Madoff's Guinness-Book-worthy Ponzi scheme. Having weathered his share of the former, Collier had always believed the latter to be reserved for the sort of white-collar pirates who, in one way or another, ultimately got what they deserved, not for folks like him, whose prosperity was the result of hard work, dedication, and an unwavering moral compass.

That is, until five months ago when Magellan's acquisition of a small Swiss chocolate company called Toujours—a move that Collier himself had spearheaded—resulted in a 500 million-dollar loss. The fact that he had managed to keep the disaster a secret so far through a series of not-quite-legal financial gymnastics was nothing short of miraculous, and he could feel his luck growing thinner by the minute. In the meantime, he'd been spending his days locked away in his office on the eighth floor of the Magellan headquarters, feeling like a death row inmate awaiting his execution. Indeed, even in spite of the grand mahogany desk and the view of the Potomac afforded by the floor-to-ceiling windows, the room had come to feel like a prison cell, the oak-paneled walls pressing in a bit more each day.

His only solace was the framed desk photo of his three-year-old grandsons Ricky and Tommy, taken the previous year during a family trip to Hilton Head. The six of them—Collier, wife Joan, son Jason, daughter-in-law Ashley, and the boys—had spent the Fourth of July at the family's beachfront condo. Collier, sixty-six, had received a stinging sunburn scampering around on the sand with the boys, but he didn't mind. Being a grandfather enlivened him in a way he hadn't expected. If fatherhood was like being thrust into a new job with no experience or training to speak of, then grandfatherhood was like paying a friendly visit to that workplace at the end of a long and successful career—rewarding in its familiarity but free of any fretting over the future. The photograph depicted the boys ankle-deep in the surf, mugging for the camera, their scrawny little bodies half-swallowed by their red *Jabber's Jungle* swim trunks, named for the kids' show about the costumed toucan who taught life lessons to a cadre of children—"Jungle Pals" they were called. Collier had never been a religious man (the few times he'd accompanied Joan to St. Sebastian's Episcopal, the sight of the massive gilded cross looming over the altar made him feel like a thief), but now he was beginning to understand the significance that unremarkable objects can take on in a crisis: if there was indeed some supreme judiciary in the universe, he could think of no better place to look than that photograph.

Whether this qualified as praying he wasn't prepared to say, but in any event this is what he was doing the morning that the man with the gun strode into the cubicle bullpen outside his door.

At first Collier figured the ruckus for another birthday celebration. The bullpen housed sixty-seven accounting drones, and the toneless choruses of the birthday song had become a daily occurrence. After a moment, he poked his head outside the office to investigate. Workers were scurrying through the maze of cubicles, business-suited folks stumbling over office chairs and crashing into desks, sending stacks of papers swirling through the air as they stampeded toward the stairwell, away from the armed man emerging from the elevator bays.

He looked to be on the far end of his forties, dressed in dingy jeans and a faded Redskins t-shirt. Collier, however, was more preoccupied by the snub nose revolver at his side. Small and black and deadly, it was the kind of weapon that a movie gangster might brandish before the hero cop blows him away in the final act. The fellow stalked into the room, making his way down the far aisle, tentative as an animal wandering into a home. If he noticed the handful of folks cowering conspicuously beneath their desks like frightened children—*Easy targets*, Collier couldn't help thinking, immediately feeling like an asshole—he ignored them. Instead, his focus appeared to be on the nameplates of the executive office doors.

By the time it dawned on Collier that the man had come here with a specific target in mind and wasn't an *active shooter*, as Magellan's mandatory safety seminar had dubbed the gun-wielding lunatics who showed up in the news at least once a week, the man had already spotted him standing motionless in his office doorway and was now heading his way.

Without looking down, the gunman sidestepped one of the large-potted office plants that had been overturned in the drones' sudden exodus, his reticence having been replaced by a cruel determination, all wild eyes and flared nostrils. Collier, however, found himself unable to move. His brain was screeching with alarm, but his muscles remained rigid with fear. The gun: he was already bracing for the shot. What else does one expect from a gun? Hell, maybe a small part of him even *wanted* it to go off. That was its sole purpose, after all, and if there was one thing Collier could say for certain at his age, it was that everything has a purpose, the gun does and so does the man who wields it.

What he could not say was who determines that purpose. Less than a year ago he would have sworn that a man carves his own path, but that was before the Toujours catastrophe.

Because Magellan had long been struggling for ways to better connect with its millennial customer base, and because a number of other companies were already eyeing the small but profitable enterprise, Collier had leaned on the legal department to hurry through the due diligence, fudging figures where needed—nothing illegal, just enough to expedite the process without raising any flags. Had they paid closer attention to the balance sheets, they might have picked up on the trail of discrepancies dating back to 2007 between accounts receivable listings and those referenced in the credit reports. But opportunity rarely favors the cautious. From time to time, it demands that you take the easy route. If you're lucky, you'll be rewarded for your leap of faith.

And if not, well, you better be able to foist it onto someone below you.

Shortly after the deal had gone through as a matter of course, he was asked by Toujours' junior operations officer Matthias Fritzl for a meeting in Zurich. "We should talk perhaps," the man said over Collier's speakerphone, his German accent lending the words a bouncy cadence. "Face-to-face is best, I am thinking."

"Why don't I just have my secretary set up a videoconference? Zurich is a hike for me."

"No," Fritzl insisted. "You must come here, Mr. Collier. It is important."

Collier was skeptical—was Fritzl even authorized to request a meeting?—but he nevertheless agreed. Probably it was just an opportunity for Toujours to show one last bit of swagger, throw a little money around. The Europeans relished any opportunity to yank the chains of American businessmen, especially when said businessmen had just gobbled up all their assets.

And so he wasn't entirely surprised when, the day after his arrival, Fritzl sauntered into the Kronenhalle Restaurant, where he had insisted that they meet, almost an hour late. The place was a formal Victorian-style establishment, with a globe chandelier and brass wall sconces. Red portiere drapes framed the plate glass windows at the front of the dining room. Collier put Fritzl somewhere in his mid-fifties. Dressed casually in a blazer and jeans, the man was a towering figure whose stringy limbs gave him the unsettling appearance of a marionette. He had a bored, standoffish air about him that reminded Collier of Jason's surly teenage years. In fact, the only time he spoke to Collier during the meal was to correct his German. "It is *kinder*, not *enfants*," the man chided when Collier fell back to gushing about his grandsons, his default small talk position. "They speak French in the west, German in the east. We are in the east, yes?"

Collier sipped his wine and fell silent. True, he didn't have a mastery of any of the country's dialects (the language CDs he'd listened to in preparation for the trip had just made him sleepy), but he was just trying to fill the silence. A little conversation didn't seem like that much to ask for, especially after having flown halfway around the planet.

And for what? The acquisition had been completed—what could this man possibly want from him? Why he had agreed to come here at all, especially under such dubious circumstances, Collier didn't know, but it made him wish that Magellan could devour the little company all over again, chew it up and swallow it like one of Toujours' own candies.

Finally, during their post-meal coffee Collier decided he'd had enough.

"Look, why am I here?"

Fritzl held his eyes for a long moment, an impish little smile playing at the corners of his mouth. He stirred some cream into his coffee and took a dainty sip.

"It is all of it made up, you know."

"What is? I don't understand know what the hell you're talking about."

"The books. All the numbers, faked."

Collier squinted at the man. "Wait a second. Which numbers do you mean? Are you talking about the earnings reports?"

"I am saying that Toujours has no money. We are broke."

Collier's gaze drifted over to the windows, the traffic trundling antlike down the crumbling Wasserwerkstrasse. Beyond it was the Limmat River, a dingy brown artery cleaving the city into halves. A sludgy film coated the surface like mold. Floes of trash bobbed against the stone levees. How had he envisioned Zurich prior to his arrival? Rustic chalets high up in the mountains maybe, champagne and foie gras by a cozy fire. Gorgeous women in skintight ski gear, blond guys in lederhosen. But now he could see that like so many other things, this place was an open cadaver, all its grisly viscera obvious beneath its imperial façade. Only up close could you see it for what it was. And as Fritzl went on to explain in his disturbingly casual tone how Toujours had been manipulating its expenses over the years to conceal its insolvency—knowing that once the acquisition went through it would be someone else's problem—Collier considered that this was the way of all things: there was never enough skin to disguise the ugliness beneath.

He leaned across the table. "Why are you just now telling me this?"

"It is my conscience. This knowledge is weighing very much on me."

"But you've had fucking *months*! Jesus, why didn't you say something sooner?"

Fritzl folded his napkin into a swan, unfolded it, and did it again. "I have a family, yes? I did not know what would happen if I told you then. The people in my business, they take things very seriously. I was told to keep quiet about it." A long, heavy pause, and then: "I am sorry,

Mr. Collier."

Gripping the edge of the table hard enough to make his knuckles ache, Collier gawped at the man as the realization seeped in: Magellan's half a billion-dollar purchase had been a waste, and there was nothing anyone could do about it. Any lawsuits filed against Toujours would most likely be thrown out in light of his own shoddy research. And while the losses carried Magellan perilously close to bankruptcy, Collier would be quietly deposed for breach of fiduciary confidence. Even if he wasn't convicted, he'd lose his CPA license and the bank would seize everything from him and Joan, the house and cars, their accounts, not to mention everything they'd set aside for Jason and Ashley and the twins. An entire life wiped clean from the ledgers.

He futzed with his silverware. "You're a goddamn coward," he hissed. His voice was as hot as steam in his throat.

"I am a man of conscience," Fritzl replied with a shrug, his froggish lips still twitching in a grin. "But I am not a man of action, I fear."

Was Collier surprised two weeks later when the junior operations officer was found dead in a Milan hotel room after having slashed his wrists with a box cutter? Not especially. At least that explained his air of detachment in the restaurant. Collier had known his share of men like Fritzl, men who were built to break. You couldn't respect them, and you certainly couldn't pity them. And yet, the news did provoke a curious spark of envy: coward or not, Fritzl possessed an intimate appreciation of purpose—specifically, that his had been served, leaving him with nothing left to offer. And to be fair, that was more than you could say for most folks.

Meanwhile, Collier was forced to begin executing his under-the-radar revenue shifts to keep the loss quiet. He syphoned from pension funds and maintenance budgets, tweaked revenue reports. He could fix this, couldn't he? Yes, he didn't have a choice. It would take some creativity, but he had the skills to recover the money. Or enough of it, anyway.

What he didn't have was time, and so when his first round of moves failed, he was forced to start cutting staff. Custodial and groundskeeping primarily, lower-end clerical folks. People whose dismissal wouldn't draw attention. To that end he was successful; as far as the rest of the company was concerned, this was just another routine round of spending reduction layoffs, regular as days of the week.

At night, to console himself, he would crawl into the Barcalounger in the basement rec room to stare blankly at the television, reassuring himself that he was no tyrant, just another working man struggling to stay afloat, which made him as much a victim as any of the folks he was letting go. Some nights he'd watch whatever happened to be on HBO; others he'd spend hours flipping absently through the channels, a glass of Scotch sweating on the table beside him, until he fell asleep with his fingers still curled around the remote.

One night he accidentally queued up one of the twins' episodes of *Jabber's Jungle*, still saved on his DVR from their last visit. Too drunk and despondent to turn it off, Collier ended up sitting through the entire thing. It was silly and artless but entertaining nonetheless, a *Barney*-style program that aspired for a kind of hipster cachet. When it was over he watched the next episode, and then another one after that, until before he knew it he was locked into a marathon, his socked toes twitching in time to all the dippy songs about picking up your toys and not talking to strangers. Just like the desk photo of his grandsons, there was something soothing about the show, its pointed lack of complexity, especially the end when Jabber would gather the half-dozen Jungle Pals together to perform a dance called the Jabber Jam over the credits. As far as Collier could tell, it involved little more than turning around in circles and waggling your hands in the air. It was so damn *simple*, that ridiculous dancing bird, the Jungle Pals following along with the manic enthusiasm of church revivalists. The Jabber Jam just made sense, he considered, not in spite of its absurdity but because of it.

Now all of this shot through Collier's mind in a momentary flash as the gunman, closing in only a few yards away, raised the weapon toward him. This close up, Collier could make out the pockets beneath his eyes, the harrowed grooves around his mouth. He had thick black eyebrows and skin the color of sandalwood. Of course, he had no way of knowing who the gunman was—Eduardo Ortiz, former custodian at the Magellan headquarters and two-time resident of the George Washington University Hospital psychiatric unit, whose job Collier had purged weeks earlier, at which point Ortiz had gone off his regimen of antipsychotics, plummeting into a homicidal fantasy world in which Collier, his name having been printed at the bottom of his termination notice, was the figurehead of a global plot to systematically destroy his life.

But as the barrel settled only inches from his nose, Collier recognized something in the man's demeanor: a dark and quavering desperation, as if he had been compelled here against his will. Hadn't he seen that same desperation on Matthias Fritzl's face five months ago, when he'd stared into the man's hooded eyes and known with nerve-rattling certainty that he had reached the end of his lifespan? Yes, and on the faces of the countless mid-level executives and directors and managers and assistant managers and team leaders and project developers and IT specialists and web designers and marketing strategists whose terminations he'd overseen during his time at Magellan, a duty he'd always regarded as an unpleasant part of an otherwise noble mission. It was the look of someone who has outlasted his usefulness.

And yet Collier wasn't afraid.

Nor was he *un*afraid, for that matter. Staring down the barrel of the revolver, he found to his astonishment that he couldn't feel anything. The moment was too immense, too *real*, to justify any emotional response.

Perhaps this was why his body now overrode his brain by summoning his hands into the air. At first it didn't even register for him what was happening, not until he noticed the gunman's eyes flick upward, puzzled, at which point Collier's hands, hanging limp-wristed over his head, began to waggle and his foot jerked forward in a little kick and then the other, and suddenly he was turning in circles, his body bobbing with each step like the needle of a metronome. He thought about Joan and Jason, and about the twins and that long weekend at the beach, their little shrieks of laughter ringing out like chimes over the wash of the surf, and even as he watched the gunman curl his finger around the trigger, Collier wasn't scared. He was a Jungle Pal now, safe on that sound stage with Jabber and the rest of the Jungle Pals and the camera trained on him, and the only thing that mattered was that he keep turning, keep turning, his fingers fluttering and his heartbeat keeping tempo, as he waited for someone off-screen to holler *Cut!*

Love, Despite its History

I've been home for all of five minutes when Cassidy calls to tell me she's just been mugged. Ten minutes later I'm swinging into the glass-littered parking lot of her apartment complex and then climbing the open-air stairwell to the third floor, not even having bothered to change out of the ridiculous skirt and stockings I'm required to wear at the Chevy dealership ("We cater to a, let's say, older-fashioned crowd," the jowly, red-nosed manager chided me on my first day as assistant media relations director when I made the mistake of wearing a pantsuit).

I knock on her door. "Abby?" she squeaks from the other side. "Is that you?"

"Yeah, it's me, Cass."

"Are you alone?"

"Yes."

"Promise?"

"Yes, sweetie, I promise."

I hear the metallic clunks of the chain, deadbolt, and sliding lock being undone, and the door opens halfway. Cassidy peeks out from behind it, her face mascara-streaked and glazed with tears. Once I'm inside, she slams it shut and locks it again and piles herself into my arms. "Abby," she sobs, burying her face in my shoulder. "Oh, Abby!"

I stroke her hair and make these little shushing noises. "It's okay," I murmur into her ear. "Just calm down. I'm here now."

After a couple minutes she manages to compose herself, and she guides me into the living room. The police have already come and gone, and now Cassidy is left with the cumbersome task of canceling her stolen credit cards, a duty that she has relegated to her boyfriend Ian, whom I'm a bit disheartened to see pacing the tiny kitchen with his phone clamped to his head: I was enjoying the idea that I was the first one she called, maybe even the only one. "No, that's what I'm telling you, it wasn't *my* card, it was my girlfriend's," he says. "She was the one who got robbed. I have all the information."

Cassidy flops down into the kiddie pool-sized papasan chair in the corner of the living room. "He's been on hold with the credit card people for like half an hour," she moans. "I told him to tell me when he gets through to someone who can help. I just can't handle it right now." This last part she emphasizes with a helpless little sweep of her hand.

Taking a seat on the adjacent sofa, I ask her to tell me what happened. She was checking her mail outside the building, she explains, when they snuck up behind her—two men, the hoods of their thick jackets cinched tight around their heads, making it impossible to see their faces in the shadowy corner of the parking lot. One of them stood off to the side a few feet keeping an eye out while the other pointed a gun at her. *Quiet*, he said, sliding her purse off her shoulder and then slinging it over his own, bored, like this was all routine, like the whole thing was just a big drag. Luckily for Cassidy, there was very little cash inside, but there was her birth control, and of course the credit cards.

"He was all like, *Hold out your arms*," Cassidy says. "And so I did, and he pushed my sleeves up, you know, looking for jewelry? They took my watch and that bracelet my dad got me, you remember?"

Wincing, I nod. Cassidy's dad is an analyst for a large electronics manufacturer, a job that involves a good deal of international travel. The bracelet—copper, with these little pea-sized indentations, perfect for Cassidy's warm skin tone—was from someplace in Mexico, a gift for her twenty-seventh birthday.

I ask her what the police told her. "They said they'd put out a bulletin but that I shouldn't get my hopes up. They said most muggings go unsolved because there's, like, never any leads."

"God, I'm so sorry." I give her knee a reassuring squeeze. "At least

that's all they took, you know? Really, it could have been a lot worse."
Inwardly, I have to cringe at the hollowness of this last part. People told
me the exact same thing after my father died abruptly of a pulmonary
embolism when I was fourteen. As if to suggest that grief was a luxury,
something you have to earn. But what else is there to tell her? Seriously,
just watch the news for five minutes. She's lucky to have walked away at
all.

"I know. It's just stuff, it can all be replaced. But still, it was *my* stuff."
With a jittery sigh, she grabs a tissue from the end table and blows her
nose. "I mean, I fucking loved that bracelet."

Ian walks in from the kitchen and holds the phone out to her like a
kid with a broken toy. "They say it has to be you, they won't let me do it
for you," he explains, seemingly baffled by the concept. "Account privacy
and stuff." He's a tall gangly ginger with a pointy face and about three feet
of ruddy forehead. Think of how Ron Howard might look after being put
through a taffy puller.

With a frustrated huff, Cassidy hoists herself out of the chair and
takes the phone and heads into the kitchen, leaving me and Ian to fumble
through another bout of halting, awkward small talk. "Hey, Abby," he
says. He shoves his hands in his pockets and begins bouncing anxiously
on the balls of his feet. "Good to see you."

"Thanks, you too."

"Wish it was under better circumstances."

"Yeah."

"You been doing okay?"

He bobs his big head nonchalantly. "Doing good, doing good. Just,
you know, working and stuff. Playing music."

"Good."

"How about you?"

"Can't complain."

"Glad to hear it."

Ian's been with Cassidy for just over six months now, and he and I still can't seem to shake our awkwardness around each other. Part of it has to do with his job: he's a pharmacy tech at Walgreen's and usually works the graveyard shift, and so we haven't spent much time together. Then there's his band, a four-piece punk outfit called The Dead Starlets. Their gimmick involves dressing up on stage like famous actresses who have died under questionable circumstances. Ian, the bassist, is Brittany Murphy. Cassidy thinks the whole thing is adorable. She's got entire Facebook albums of Ian donning his halter, blonde wig, and globby ringlets of mascara. To me, it all seems unmistakably juvenile, loaded with the kind of Freudian innuendos one might ascribe to serial killers. But what the hell do I know? I cater to an older-fashioned crowd.

We both fall quiet and glance toward the kitchen, desperately willing Cassidy to return. To fill the silence, I ask Ian if he's working tonight. He ceases his bouncing, looking suddenly serious. "Yeah, see that's kind of the thing. The boss let me pop over here to make sure Cassidy was okay, but I'm sort of covering someone else's shift right now, so I gotta get back in a little bit."

"Gotcha."

"Look, I really don't think she should be by herself tonight, under the circumstances, I mean. Is there any way you could crash here or something?"

I cast a brief look past him toward the kitchen, where Cassidy is tearfully giving the credit card rep her contact information, looking as helpless as a child, as she usually does in moments of duress.

"Yeah, I guess I can do that."

"Seriously? You don't mind?"

"Nah, I don't mind," I reply, picking a piece of lint off my skirt. I pretend to examine it, then flick it away. "Someone needs to be here with her."

Ian thanks me, gives me a brief businesslike shoulder squeeze, and trots into the kitchen to check on Cassidy. Whether he chose to disregard the subtle recrimination in this last part or if he missed it altogether, I can't be sure.

After Ian has left, I pour a couple glasses of wine for me and Cassidy and help her wipe the mascara off her cheeks. I turn on *American Idol*, but we're too wired to pay attention. Instead, I listen patiently as she vents about the ordeal. Every so often I'll toss out an obligatory "I know" or "You're right" or "That makes sense."

"How much do you want to bet they live there, in my fucking complex?" she says. "I mean, do you think they *knew* me? Like, they've seen me before and know what time I get home and all that? This little white chick living all by herself?" Sniffling, she grabs another Kleenex and blows her nose. The coffee table is a wasteland of balled-up tissues.

"I don't know, sweetie. Maybe."

Actually, I'm almost certain of this. How else would they have known to corner her there? Cassidy's complex is a sad collection of humble brick buildings in a section of town rarely frequented by those who can afford to avoid it. The stairwells are mottled with graffiti, and at night it's not uncommon to hear violent arguments erupting from inside. The parking lot is always full of saggy-panted young men blaring car stereos. The upside is that this place is only a twenty-minute walk to her job at CityArts, a nonprofit artists' conglomeration that repurposes garbage for functional art projects around town—benches made from recycled car parts, light fixtures crafted from shards of bottle glass, that sort of thing. She's the PR rep, a job that seems to entail little more than soliciting recycling centers and junkyards for materials.

As for the muggers, my guess is that they had zeroed in on Cassidy's air of subservience. I suppose this is what you'd expect from someone who's spent nearly three decades being the prettiest girl in the room, the queen bee, the girl to whom the rest of us so eagerly flock, hoping to be absorbed into her aura of sensual poise. She's a petite blonde, slender but not in that gross sickly way, with thick curls that fall prettily over her ears, emphasizing her delicate doll-like features. Bee-stung lips. Eyes as big and blue as something out of a cartoon. Hers is the kind of brutal hopeless beauty that makes you want to swoop in and save her from the horrors of the world.

Then there's me, with my oversized ears and nose and my thick, sturdy, unfeminine frame. Somehow we've managed to stay friends all these years, even after the rest of our friends got married and retreated to the suburbs and started plastering the back windows of their minivans with stick-figure children. Lucky for her I have a history of looking after fragile women. It's a skill I honed after Dad died, leaving me to take care of my younger sister Amanda, twelve at the time, and my mother, who coped with his death by isolating herself in her bedroom for the next six years with a bottle of vodka and a regimen of painkillers. For the first few months, relatives would pop in regularly to assist with grocery shopping and yard work. But then after a couple days when they satisfied their sense of familial obligation, they'd be gone again. Mom, meanwhile, deteriorated from a pert, upbeat woman with a body made toned and shapely from years of marathon running, to a sullen, leathery-faced creature who slept up to twenty hours a day. To see her sulking around the house in my father's dingy blue robe, her once lush auburn hair now thin and brittle, you might have mistaken her for a chemotherapy patient. As for Amanda, I was able to delegate some of the chores to her, but there's only so much you can expect from a mourning preteen, especially one whose coping mechanisms involved keying the neighbors' cars and giving blowjobs on the school bus.

Is it any wonder, then, that I would gravitate toward Cassidy in college? She was new and exciting, the kind of person I always aspired to be. In addition to living only a few doors down from each other in the freshman dorm, we shared a couple classes—we were both public relations majors—including Intro to Statistics, for which I tutored her. We'd meet up in the library, and with the tenderness of a kindergarten teacher I would guide her through the practice problems in the book. "God, I am *so* not a numbers person," she'd complain, always inches from a sob. "I'm never going to get this shit. I'm so dumb."

"You're not dumb, it's hard stuff," I'd reply reassuringly, despite having long ago resigned myself to the fact that math and all its variations were generally the territory of those of us whose looks would never be our livelihood. And so when she eked by with a C- (a monumental achievement for her), I swallowed her in a hug and told her I'd known all along that she could do it.

According to its website, Many Villages is a fair trade retailer specializing in unique handmade jewelry and gifts from around the world. The shop is small and musty and crammed full of rainsticks and badly painted teakwood furniture.

"I'm—I'm not sure what you're talking about," says the salesgirl, wrinkling her pointy studded nose. "This was a bracelet, you said?"

"Yes. Copper, with these little, I don't know, indentations all over it."

"Indentations?"

"Right. It's maybe this wide." I hold my fingers about an inch apart.

"Huh." She puzzles over the description. She's got dyed black hair and enough jewelry in her face to stock a display case at Zale's. "I mean, we have some copper pieces, if you wanna look. We've got—"

"If you can show me a catalog or something, I can probably find it for you."

Sighing, she rolls her eyes. "Yeah, okay, we don't sell mass-produced stuff." Her voice oozes with disdain. "It's all handmade, one-of-a-kind. Sometimes there's, like, multiple versions of one thing, but never like the exact same thing."

I glance around the cluttered showroom. Feebly, I mutter, "It's from Mexico."

I sleep on Cassidy's couch the night after the mugging, and then the night after that, until by the end of the week the three of us, me and her and Ian, have fallen into a cozy domestic rhythm: in the mornings when Ian arrives home from the pharmacy, before Cassidy and I head off to work, I'll whip up some breakfast, and we will pack ourselves in around the small kitchen table to eat. It's a nice little routine, comfortable and homey, even in spite of Ian's continual griping about how, like, *tired* he is, and how, like, *exhausting* the graveyard shift can be—complaints that always seemed directed at me, as though I'm partially at fault for his exhaustion. Still, I like to think that to anyone looking in on the three of us buttering toast and passing the OJ back and forth, we might resemble an actual family.

But then there's always the inevitable before-work retreat to my apartment to drop off my dirty clothes and water my dying plants, where the empty silence of the place, rudely contrasted by the squeals and chuffs of the city buses outside my window, only reinforces the fact of my loneliness. It reminds me that nearly all of the people I care about have gone away in one manner or another, that this is the natural progression of things: your world whittles itself down to a fine point, and if you're lucky what's left will be just enough to sustain you until the end.

The Dead Starlets are playing at this little Irish pub that Cassidy and I used to frequent back in school. We're sitting at a small table near the bar, listening to the band plow through their roster of screamy, galloping tunes. Cassidy's on her third Cosmo—her customary night-out drink—drunkenly pounding the table in time to the music. And good for her, really. It's been two weeks since the mugging, and she's needed to blow off some steam.

As for me, I'm nursing a watered-down gin and tonic, pretending to appreciate the sweaty, cross-dressed spectacle on stage and trying not to notice the trio of spiky-haired boys who've been whooping it up at the bar a few feet away, falling over each other with big clumsy guffaws, glancing over their shoulders to see if we've noticed them. It makes me think of nights out in college with our small cohort of girlfriends, how we could always count on at least a couple rounds of drinks being sent to our table, and how hard we had to work to mask our exhilaration. Deep down we all understood that they were actually meant for Cassidy and not the rest of us, but we were happy to ignore this understanding if it meant getting to feel desirable, at least for a little while.

The band finishes the song and Cassidy, already half-sloshed, claps fiercely. "Woohoo! Good job, baby!" To me she says, "God, aren't they *good*?"

I nod with manufactured enthusiasm. I'd rather listen to a lawnmower. Once the ringing in my ears has subsided, I say, "So, any news from the police?"

She tosses back the last of her drink. "No. I've called a couple times, but it's like, what can they do, you know? I couldn't even see the guys' faces." She motions to the waitress for another round of drinks. "I'm trying to get out of my lease."

"You're moving?"

"Not sure yet. That place is just so super skeezy. I want to live somewhere I at least feel safe."

I trace the key-carved graffiti in the tabletop: *Tammy Shaw sux dik.*

"I told you that when you moved in. Don't you remember me saying you shouldn't settle for someplace unsafe?"

"Yeah yeah, fine," she says, twisting a straw wrapper around her finger, "You were right, *Mom*."

Another round of laughter from the jackals at the bar. Instinctively we look over, a mistake. One of them, this tall dude with frosted blonde hair and tattoo sleeves, has angled himself in his seat so that he's facing us. He might be cute if it weren't for his outfit: tight jeans and one of those black muscle shirts that looks like something a rugged movie hero might tear off before boffing the busty female lead. The bad boy look, about as titillating as a onesie. His slow gaze, full of greedy appraisal, settles upon me like a searchlight.

Cassidy leans across the table and, in a deep mocking register, says, "Oh, dude, I am *so* gonna tap that tonight."

"Killer, bro. Then let's go play frisbee with our shirts off."

"Okay, but first I have to Photoshop biceps on my profile pic, dawg."

We cackle with laughter. Sensing that we're making fun of them, the men turn back around toward the bar.

Three songs into the band's second set, Cassidy's so drunk she can barely hold her head up. "Think Ian'll be pissed?" she says as I steer her past the bar, hoisting her up beneath the arms, toward the exit at the front of the pub.

"I don't think so. He's pretty understanding."

As we round the corner of the bar she stumbles and down we go, toppling onto the sticky tile floor. The guys at the bar burst into hearty laughter.

"Need some help there?" says Tattoos.

"I think I'm good, thanks."

"I bet you are," he slurs, angling his thin lips into that snotty smirk again.

"Pfft," Cassidy snorts, firing off a few droplets of spittle. "Go on home, little boy. It's past your bedtime." She shoots him the finger. As we fumble out the door, I take one last glance over my shoulder and see that he's still grinning at me.

Cassidy spends most of the drive back to her place with her head hanging out of the car window, trying not to puke. Her hair flaps in the wind like the remnants of a tattered flag. As soon as we've made it home, she shambles into the bathroom and collapses in front of the toilet and unloads about a hundred dollars' worth of booze. I hold her sweaty hair back while she retches and heaves, as I've done at least a dozen times in the past without complaint. Taking a washcloth from the tub basin, I lean over and wipe the gobs of off-color spit from her mouth. "Need mouthwash," she groans. I fetch her the large green bottle of Scope from the sink. She swishes her mouth out and tries to prop herself up but falls back against the wall. I trot out to the kitchen and fetch a cup for her to spit into.

Peering up at me, her bloodshot eyes half-open, she grumbles, "We're too old to do this." The words seem to fall haphazardly from her lips, but her expression is one of disarming openness, like an attention-starved house pet. If she were a dog, I'd scratch her between her ears.

"I don't know about all that. We're still young."

"Not young enough."

"Young enough for what?"

But she just closes her eyes and lets her head fall to the side, and it's hard not to think about my mother, bed-ridden with grief, the deep cruel lines of her face, the pallid peaks and clefts. *Please get up*, I'd plead quietly, standing over her at her bedside. *We need you to get up. Please.*

But she would only respond with a sad, distant smile. *My pretty girl*, she'd whisper, brushing my hair back from my face, the gentleness of her voice suggesting that she found my naivety endearing, quaint. *Oh my pretty pretty girl.*

By the time Ian makes it home, still wearing his leather mini, electric blue tube top, and fishnets, I've already piled Cassidy into her bed and scrubbed the bathroom and have settled in front of the television. "How is she?" he asks, setting his guitar case down in front of the coffee table.

"Asleep."

"She alright? Did she get sick?"

"She's fine."

"Well that's good. Thanks for getting her home."

"Sure."

He moves into the middle of the living room, the gray stink of the bar hanging around him in a cloud. With his hands on his hips, he gives me this tight little smile like a waiter trying to pacify an unruly customer. "So you want me to walk you to your car or something?"

"Walk me to my car?"

"Uh-huh."

A few seconds of dense silence passes between us. "Actually, Ian, I sorta thought I would crash here again. For Cass, you know?"

Ian, looking at the floor now, nods gravely. He makes this sucking sound through his teeth.

"It's just that you've been staying over here kind of a lot."

"Yeah? So?"

"So, I mean, don't you miss your apartment? Your own bed?"

"She got *mugged*," I rebut. "At *gunpoint*."

"Yeah, I know, Abby. She called me too, remember?"

"And besides, you were the one who asked me to stay here in the first place. You remember that? So Cass wouldn't have to be alone?"

"I do. But it's been a couple of weeks already."

"Well, Ian, sometimes you have to put yourself out for the people you care about. That's how friendship works."

"Right," he chuckles, easing down into the papasan chair. "I'm sure it's a huge drag for you."

Switching off the television, I slap the remote down on the coffee table.

"Meaning what?"

"Nothing. Forget it."

"No, really. What are you saying here?"

He begins untying the ballet lacings of his four-inch wedges, his movements slow and calm like he's trying to taunt me. "I just think maybe you've done all you can do for her," he says in an even tone. With the shoes off, he sits back in the chair and offers me a smug grin. "It's nice that you want to be a good friend or whatever, but come on. At some point it's not even about friendship anymore."

I scour department stores and flea markets and museum gift shops in search of a new bracelet for Cassidy. I grill the elderly proprietors of moldy consignment stores. Riffle through bargain bins. Surf the websites of indie jewelry retailers until my eyes throb. But nothing.

Until one afternoon an hour into a search on my computer at work, when suddenly there it is: *texturized anticlassic copper cuff bracelet, $85.00*. It's identical to Cassidy's, right down to the little bowl-shaped indentations. The website is for a Mexico City-based company. With expedited shipping, the total comes to nearly $130.00. Rationally, I can't justify spending that much on a piece of jewelry, not if I want to pay bills this month and continue working toward improving my lackluster credit, but right now those things seem like secondary concerns to Cassidy's reaction, which I'm envisioning as a spectacle of ecstatic squeals and tears.

I enter my mailing information and click the Pay button.

Then somehow it's my twenty-ninth birthday, and Cassidy and I are out to dinner at one of these overpriced Japanese places where they cook your meal right in front of you. We're seated around this small grill, the two of us and a few other couples who seem mildly annoyed by our revelry. We cheer as the chef tosses and chops and sears our food, a culinary ninja. The Dead Starlets are at practice until eight and then Ian has to work, which is just fine with me. I've been snubbing him since our confrontation the other night. At Cassidy's we remain cordial for her sake but otherwise hardly speak. For his part, Ian has been particularly breezy about the whole thing, giving me these wry smiles from across the room, as though he knows something I don't.

But I'm not even thinking about that tonight. What I am thinking about is the bracelet in my jacket pocket. It arrived yesterday, and my plan is to present it to Cassidy later on in the evening, to watch her face go blank the way it does when she's genuinely taken by surprise. Show her who's really looking out for her. And if she's so touched by the gesture—the realization that after her life's inevitable self-whittling I'll be what's left—that she begins to weep?

Well, I'd be okay with that.

After dinner we make our way down the sidewalk past the glowing cavalcade of restaurants and bodegas. The cold evening wind rolls up the street, stirring the trash in the gutters and carrying the smells of spoiled food and grease. Cars fly past in bursts of frosty wind, stereos thumping. Oddly, I think back to my tenth birthday party. There was a small party at our house, just a few girls from my school, pizza and soda, that kind of thing. I remember my mom standing out on the back porch in a navy cardigan, setting out paper plates and stacks of napkins and plastic cups, and I remember her and my dad carrying my birthday cake out together, moving with these small cautious steps, trying to keep the candles from going out. I remember Amanda scurrying around in the yard, vying for the partygoers' attention. And I remember the sugary tang of the honeysuckle growing around the porch and the cool, complicated scent of my father's cologne. In only a few years, Dad would be gone and Mom would become whatever it is that people turn into when the soul decays, haunting our sad little house in a boozy cloud, her skin taking on the acid stink of rotting fruit. A pale spectral reminder of what the world ultimately has to offer.

Cassidy, wearing a knee-length leather coat and red knit hat, puts her arm through my mine and leans into me, shivering theatrically. "Okay, someone turn off the cold. I'm ready for summer."

"It's only December. You've got a while, hon."

"You're a goddamn buzzkill."

We arrive at a club where some of the guys from CityArts have already convened, well-coifed gay men with bodies as sleek and sculpted as weapons. Cassidy squeezes my shoulders. "My girl is one year closer to menopause!" she announces.

Within minutes drinks begin appearing in front of me on the table, colorful concoctions that sound like they've been named after low-budget porno flicks. Screaming Orgasm. Sex on the Beach. Red-Headed Slut. The men laugh and cheer as I throw each one back, as though there's something at stake here. And who knows, maybe there is.

Finally, during a lull in the revelry, when it's just me and Cass next to each other at the table, I reach into my pocket to retrieve the bracelet.

But before I'm able to present it to her she says, matter-of-factly, "So, they let me out of my lease."

"Yeah?"

"Yeah. I'm moving in with Ian."

I freeze, mouth open, fingertips poised on the bracelet's dimpled surface.

"You are?"

"Yeah. Pretty grownup of me, huh?" She sniggers.

"But that's all the way across town. It's like a forty-five minute drive."

"I know. That part does kind of suck. I love being able to walk to work. But it's a two-birds-one-stone thing. I get to leave my place, and honestly I think this is a good move for me and him right now." Resting her chin in her hand, she says in a pretend-dreary voice, "We all gotta settle down eventually, right?"

There's a glass of something pink and syrupy-looking in front of me. I swallow the remainder of it and then sit back, my head bonking the wall behind me. Something has gone wrong here, I'm just not sure what.

"What about me?" I hear myself say.

"What? The music, I can't hear you."

"What about me? You could live with me. In my place."

Her smile falters as if a tendon in her face has snapped.

"Oh. Well, I mean, that's really sweet of you, Abby. It's just that, um, you know, this feels like something we need to do, me and Ian."

"But why?" I sputter, reaching for her hand, and there must be something desperate in my voice because Cassidy leans away from me, her frown deepening. "*Why* do you need to? Is it just because you're scared? That's why you're doing it, isn't it? Because you don't want to be alone?"

"I'm doing it"—she yanks her hand out of my grip, a crisp edge in her voice—"because I *want* to. We *want* to be together. What the fuck, Abby? I don't get why you're being weird about this."

Nor, for that matter, do I, and yet I can feel an unmooring inside me, something drifting out of reach. For a few moments all I can do is stare at her, waiting for the right words to come to mind. When they don't, I leap out of the booth and elbow my way toward the bathrooms. Cassidy says something to my back, but I ignore it. The music, suddenly a violent pulsing force compelling me through the crush of perfumed bodies. The dizzying heat of the alcohol, the booming voices all around me. All I want is to go home and sleep and spend the rest of my birthday in drunken silence.

And wouldn't you know it that as I slip around a booth, I bump right into Tattoos. It takes him a moment to recognize me from the pub, but then suddenly he's giving me that absurd sideways grin, all thin lips and dimples. "Hey, hey," he says. "Look who—"

Grabbing him by the collar of his V-neck t-shirt, I pull myself to him and kiss him. He grunts in surprise but doesn't protest. All at once we're tangled together, fumbling backward through the crowd until we hit the back wall, his hands gripping my ass, pushing himself into my midsection so hard that it hurts, grinding the bracelet into my hipbone, our mouths working against each other with a kind of violent appetite.

We stagger into one of the men's room stalls. The stench is thick enough to choke on, but that doesn't stop him from clawing away at my zipper, and it doesn't stop me from letting him, and suddenly I know that whatever happens next was always going to happen, there was never any way to stop it. Just like Dad's embolism, just like Cassidy's mugging. Don't let anyone tell you there are no guarantees. *Everything* is a guarantee.

Now here's Tattoos spinning me around, clamping his clammy hands on my hips with an urgency that should be more alarming than it is, except we're past all that now, past whatever it is we're supposed to feel, and as he's tugging as the waistband of my skirt he manages to dislodge the bracelet from my pocket. It clinks onto the tiled floor like an unanswered plea. With a disembodied numbness I stare at the thing, wondering about whichever man happens to spot it laying there by the grimy drain. What will go through his head? Will he speculate about the girl who dropped it, how she found herself in such a place? And will he ask himself why she didn't bother to pick it up?

At the Bottom of Everything

Today is the one-year anniversary of the Conway High Massacre, as it
has come to be called, and we, the nineteen surviving gunshot victims,
have converged on the large desolate field where Travis Covington,
seventeen, filmed his now-infamous video diary before opening fire on
a pep rally in the Conway High School gymnasium, killing twenty-six.
It's midnight, and the crisp night air is rich with the aromas of earth and
grass and decay. Our feet send up a chorus of inelegant squishing sounds
as we proceed into the mud, sidestepping pieces of junk deposited by
neighborhood residents unwilling to make the trek to the dump across
town: broken appliances, tattered furniture, mounds of old mildewed
clothes. A graveyard of possibilities. With our eyes fixed on the ground
in search of rusty metal scraps, we might appear to onlookers like a
search party combing the area for a missing person.

Actually, what we are looking for is the baseball diamond-sized
pond on the far side of the field where Travis used to practice shooting
at beer bottles. Even before the video diary was released, everyone in the
area was familiar with the field, though it is large enough that finding the
pond—in the dark, no less—proves difficult; in fact, the diary, Fedexed
to WKLG News an hour before the attack, gave little indication of its
location amidst the weedy, garbage-strewn expanse. In the video, Travis
would set the bottles to float in the center by way of a small platform
constructed from plastic containers. The viewer can see the bottles
pop and shatter in mists of brown glass. In the wake of the attack, the
footage went viral, attracting scads of gawkers to the site, eventually
forcing police to cordon off the area until the traffic stopped altogether.
Up until now we have avoided the field, partially for this reason, but
mostly out of a childish fear that our presence might be met with the
ghostly vengeance reserved for movie characters who have stumbled

upon ancient Indian burial grounds.

Classes will end at one o'clock today for what promises to be a sobering commemorative assembly in the front of the school. The mayor will speak, and then a few words from student council president Jessica Schiff, and then principal Moody will call for twenty-six seconds of silence. We will be seated in a row of folding chairs at the front, dressed in our honorary CHS letter jackets, of course, hands folded in our laps like penitents, exuding the heroic poise that has come to be expected of us. It's not so hard to understand why our classmates would like our scars to Mean Something, to "emblemize the triumph of the human spirit," as one slick-haired South Carolina senator phrased it. Who doesn't want to rationalize their traumas, if only to preserve their conception of the universe as an ordered system in which righteousness and evil are easily distinguishable?

It is for their sakes, then, that we have kept the truth to ourselves: that there is no meaning to be gleaned from our scars, no arcane wisdom, only a cold, sinister reminder that at best everything is only temporary. Even us.

Maybe this is why our hands instinctively seek out our scars as we approach the pond, the calm surface sparkling plaintively in the moonlight. Notice, for instance, how Emily Lepisto clasps her left wrist, feeling the twin dimples from the slug that left her unable to bend her fingers more than a few degrees. Or see Adam Kravski remove his Clemson cap and absent-mindedly trace the mottled pink ridges crisscrossing his head, making his skull look like a Phillips' head screw. Altogether we carry 5.8 pounds of titanium alloys in the form of cranial plates, bone screws, artificial knee caps, and spinal fusion cages. So far we have undergone a total of seventy-one surgeries to repair punctured lungs, perforated bowels, temporal bone fractures, cerebral contusions, pulmonary lacerations, intracranial hematomas, arteriovenous fistulas, hemothorax, periocardial tamponade. Three of us have suffered neurological impairments that, while thankfully having no effect on our cognitive abilities, will prevent us from ever driving again. One of us is now blind in one eye.

The most iconic clip from the video diary features Travis standing with his back to the pond, dressed in a black t-shirt and cargo pants, clutching the weapon, a Bushmaster .223 semiautomatic rifle purchased online with a fake ID, to his tawny chest. "This is my manifesto," he says robotically into the tripod-mounted camera. "For too long I have been ridiculed and tormented. Now the guilty must pay, the fakes and the liars. You brought this on yourselves."

It is this clip alone that has allowed him in our memories to take on the impossible dimensions of a mythical figure—half human, half speculation, a harsh contrast to the nervous, lanky, fair-skinned boy we'd see skulking through the halls like a death row inmate on his way to the gas chamber. He was never very popular outside of his cohort of friends, with whom he usually spent his lunch hour playing Jenga in the AV lab. With their bad skin and anime t-shirts, they all seemed interminably trapped on the edge of adolescence in a way that made them outcasts, foreigners amongst the rest of us. Beyond this, we knew almost nothing about his personal life, other than that he had an older sister, Tori, who had graduated before any of us had started high school but whose promiscuity remained something of a legend amongst the students. (She was rumored to have once taken part in a house party game to see which of five girls could fellate the most boys in a half hour and, as a consequence, had to have her stomach pumped of semen; that no one was ever able to verify this did not stop us from trading the story time and again like gospel.) His parents, we learned after the attack, had been divorced for most of his life; his mother was a paralegal in Conway, and his father had a wife and two other children and owned a four-wheeler dealership in New Orleans.

But it's the seemingly innocuous memories of Travis that have taken on the most retrospective weight in our minds. Whitney Smith remembers when he chose *Mein Kampf* for his end-of-the-year research project in sophomore English, and how annoyed Janice Arendale was when it took first prize in the annual CHS Writing Contest, beating out her sonnet about her family trip to Mexico ("He only chose that book to get attention," she was overheard complaining to a classmate). Kevin Molarno recalls the two straight weeks he wore sunglasses for no apparent reason, and how he used to draw flames on his tennis shoes. Brian Vick remembers when, during a fetal pig dissection in his sophomore bio lab, he began to dry heave into the sink and had to be escorted by Mrs. Odell into the hall, where he spent the remainder of the period sobbing hysterically.

Maybe these were nothing more than the hallmarks of awkward adolescence; we were all teenagers, after all, gloomy in our own ways and terrified of what the world had to offer. Nevertheless, in our minds they now seem hopelessly laden with significance, like opportunities that only reveal themselves once you've missed them.

On the September morning in question, he strode into the gym with the rifle in his hands just as the dance team was finishing up a routine. "We didn't know what we were seeing, not at first," DeShaun Burgess would later comment in a CNN news feed. "We all thought maybe it was, like, part of a skit or something." Coach Barnes, an Iraq War vet (the fact of which has received almost as much coverage as the shooting itself, not to mention whispers of a made-for-TV-movie option) was the first to realize what was happening. Leaping up from the bleachers, he yelled "Get down!" and then darted across the court toward Travis, presumably with the intention of tackling him. Travis, clad in the same black paramilitary garb he'd worn in the video diary, took aim and, with an eerie calm, shot the coach through the right eye. The man's head snapped back violently as if yanked by an invisible string, and he dropped to the floor in mid-step. At least three radio talk show hosts would make comparisons to the Kennedy assassination.

A chorus of terrified screams rose up from the bleachers. Students flooded the floor all at once, clamoring for the exits, tripping and trampling each other, despite the teachers' frantic attempts to corral them into the halls. The thick pops of the rifle resounded throughout the room, big as planets, while all around us it seemed bodies were collapsing, shredded by gunfire. The scorched smell of cordite, the panicked tang of sweat. For some of us, like Katie Wilkes, the blasts hit with enough scalding force to send us flying off our feet. Others didn't even realize at first that we had been hit, as in the case of Doug Castalabri, who, propelled by adrenaline and fear, assumed the blood on his shirt was someone else's, until once outside the building he noticed the dime-sized hole in his abdomen.

Altogether, Travis Covington fired off seventy-four rounds in approximately 3.2 minutes before turning the gun on himself. Ballistics reports would later describe the shooting pattern as "random and uncoordinated." The video diary was aired by every major news network in the country, and Travis, who hadn't had the stomach to make it through a fetal pig dissection, became one of the most popular search terms online for nearly four weeks straight.

As for possible motives, people have suggested maybe video games drove him to it, or the absence of his father, or milk hormones, or perhaps even his ADD, but who can ever know these things? That's the worst part, really, trying to find a singular cause while knowing at the same time that such things don't exist. Aren't we naturally predisposed to believe, despite all reason, that tragedy serves some higher moral function? Isn't that what this afternoon's assembly is all about?

But no: tragedy has the same point of origin as everything else, and searching for it only makes you understand how little your own survival actually accomplishes.

And so this is why now, standing at the mucky edge of the pond with the reeds swishing gently against our ankles, we begin to undress, each of us without a word, because we have nothing left to hide—perhaps we never did in the first place. The cool air slides over our skins like strangers' fingertips in a crowd, arousing the fine hairs on our arms and legs. Leaving our clothes in piles in the grass, we wade chastely into the frigid water.

In the brittle moonlight, our bare bodies glow spectrally, our scars rendered practically invisible. Could this be all that healing amounts to, outlasting whatever you thought was keeping you safe? Moving farther out into the pond, we think about the video diary. We remember the footage of Travis' target practice sessions, and we imagine the bottom of the pond as a vast carpet of glass shards waiting to slice the feet of unsuspecting swimmers. Just like the childhood monsters beneath our beds, because isn't that where the danger always lives, at the bottom of everything? Hidden, but closer than anyone would like to believe.

You brought this on yourselves.

Now we lie back in the water and close our eyes and drift listlessly out toward the center of the pond. We are alone here and the night is silent save for the trilling of crickets and the wind against the grass and the water lapping gently at our goose-rippled skins. We float like corpses, the nineteen of us, wholly exposed, limbs splayed like the points of stars as we wait for whatever is beneath us to reveal itself.

ACKNOWLEDGMENTS

The stories in this collection first appeared in the following publications:

Alaska Quarterly Review: "The Fence"

Big Muddy: "In the Jungle"
(winner of the 2017 Mighty River Short Story Contest)

Delmarva Review: "The Future is Not for Sale"
(winner of the 2017 Chesapeake Voices Fiction Contest)

Green Briar Review: "Oceanography"

Hamilton Arts & Letters: "Love, Despite its History"

Indiana Review: "Birding for Beginners"

Mid-American Review: "Robo Warrior"

Packinghouse Review: "Monsters"

Shenandoah: "At the Bottom of Everything"

storySouth: "Retreat"

Special thanks for their support goes to the South Carolina Arts Commission, the Library of Virginia, Coastal Carolina University, the Virginia Tech Department of English, Southeast Missouri State University, Joe Oestreich, and Dr. Dan Albergotti.

For their assistance with these stories, I wish to thank Ed Falco, Weston Cutter, Carrie Meadows, Nick Kocz, Manisha Sharma, Ryan Shelley, Hill Powell, Beth Barber, Nancy Frowert, Brian Druckenmiller, and Pat Siebel.

I am indebted to the following for helping to keep me sane during the writing process: Neil Norman, Sally and Travis Leitko, Sean Kelly, Officers Vince Daus & Meika Fields, Brice & Maggie Harrington, Mark Spewak & Liz Grant-Spewak, Brian & Kelly Shiplov, Cliff Sosis, Colin Burch, and Robbie & Nora Hamilton.

To the staff at Orison Books—particularly Luke Hankins, Kevin McIlvoy, and Chris Hale—and to Lan Samantha Chang, I offer my most sincere gratitude. Also thanks to John Defresne, Steve Yarborough, and Michael Czyzniejewski.

Thank you, too, to my parents, Linda and Dixie Griffin.

And thanks most of all to Karen and Alex Griffin, who make the work worthwhile.

About the Author

Jeremy Griffin is originally from Louisiana. He received his MFA in Fiction from Virginia Tech University. He is the author of *A Last Resort for Desperate People: Stories and a Novella* (Stephen F. Austin University Press). He has received support from the South Carolina Arts Commission, and he teaches at Coastal Carolina University, where he serves as faculty fiction editor of *Waccamaw: A Journal of Contemporary Literature*. He lives in Myrtle Beach with his wife and son.

About Orison Books

Orison Books is a 501(c)3 non-profit literary press focused on the life of the spirit from a broad and inclusive range of perspectives. We seek to publish books of exceptional poetry, fiction, and non-fiction from perspectives spanning the spectrum of spiritual and religious thought, ethnicity, gender identity, and sexual orientation.

As a non-profit literary press, Orison Books depends on the support of donors. To find out more about our mission and our books, or to make a donation, please visit www.orisonbooks.com.